HOSPITALITY WAS NEVER LIKE THIS...

Praise For *Hotel Noir*

"I'm thoroughly intrigued by this novel, though not necessarily for straightforward reasons. I think what has hooked me is that it doesn't seem like anything else. Casper Silk has a wholly unique voice. It's an entirely bizarre one, too, and *Hotel Noir* is a dark yet evocative portrait of an island quickly changing, a hotel of another era, and a man caught in the midst, still suffering over the long-ago death of his wife, trying to help a young girl, and falling through the cracks that society allows to widen as the times change."

Lexy Bloom

Who Is Casper Silk?

Keep a secret?

Casper Silk is the pseudonym of an award-winning author whose works defy easy categorization, combining elements of literary and genre fiction, and straying from the straight-and-narrow of chronology into a kaleidoscopic striptease of the human soul.

Readers throughout the ages have made a sport of unmasking pseudonymous authors, and the rumor mill is already churning out identities for the enigmatic Silk.

So, who is Casper Silk? We're not at liberty to say—yet. But here's a hint: there is a long tradition of female authors adopting male pen names. And another: the author in question has a body of work critics have variously called "lyrical," "heart-wrenching," and "heroic."

By any name Silk delivers what readers lust after: a great read.

HOTEL NOIR

CASPER SILK

Pale Fire
Press

First Print Edition

Library of Congress Control Number: 2012906508

ISBN: 978-0-9838612-2-5

Hotel Noir online: http://palefirepress.com

For information about subsidiary rights, bulk purchases or author events, contact biz@palefirepress.com

To the Francis Steins of the world,
people of conscience and heart who
occasionally falter

To the Bat Manleys of the world, who
would like to be ruthless but suffer
from too much decency

For Aunt Marilyn, Rusty,
David and Jeannine

"Can a man take fire in his bosom,
and his clothes not burn?"

Proverbs 6.27

FRANCIS

Night at the Hotel Noir. At the Hotel Noir it is always night. The epicureans, sun worshippers and crooks that comprise her clientele rarely stir here in daytime; they are sleeping off hangovers, smothering in dreams. Open the shades and they shrink from the light, such harsh light in these tropics.

The proprietress, Guinevere Baldi Blanc, applies fresh cucumber slices to her eyes after each meal. She wears red hats, orange hats, purple hats with brims the size of parasols. She is not from this place, lacks pigment. Her husband, they say, bought her from a pimp on the outskirts of Marseilles. These days he is seldom seen in her company, seldom seen at all, but every so often one hears his commanding double handclap, sole reminder of his rule over the affable slow-moving staff.

The hotel, once the finest on St. Germaine, has dropped category in recent years. Gone the lust-struck heiresses and dethroned royals. Gone the red carpet and white gloves. The upholstery has grown greasy with tanning oil; the ceiling fans whine; the begonias sag. A blind soothsayer feels her way through the lobby, telling fortunes for the price of a meal.

I am a witness to the decay, having wintered at the Noir for twenty-five consecutive years—except for the winter of '82, when I lost track of time. Brett Foster McCabe was murdered here that New Year's Eve, still wearing his paper party hat and too drunk to feel the knife thrust. McCabe, like most, had come to the island to chase women and throw his money around. His murder was not personal, simply the natives' way of controlling the tourist population. An occasional knifing tends to scare people off for a season or two.

Until promoters lure them back with cheaper room rates and easier vice.

There seems little hope for St. Germaine. Every year her waters grow more murky, her boulevards and golf courses more unkempt, and the very people who vow to save her— politicians, developers, evangelists—sink her deeper in debt and set the citizenry at one another's throats.

Yet each November, something—a melancholy wind, the sense memory of frangipani blossoms—draws me back to the doomed little island. I check into the Hotel Noir, where my suite is always ready and the barman remembers to add a second olive to my martini. Apprised of my arrival, Madame Blanc sweeps through the lobby in one of her riotous *chapeaux* to plant the two obligatory pecks on my cheeks. Her stock greeting: "But how pale you are!" Each year finds the proprietress less of a hostess and more of a tyrant. Pity the guest who dares to track sand into her foyer, pity the lackey who chips a teacup or who leaves a crumb on the starched white tablecloths.

I have learned to avoid her—not difficult to do, given her penchant for daylong siestas. Only on Thursday evenings do I willingly enter her presence to attend the weekly salon.

It was at the salon that I met the one and only friend I have on St. Germaine, Hugo "Scar Face" Fey, who calls himself an exile though he was born in this chain of islands a mere latitude degree south. Hugo earned my devotion with a single well-timed quip. A Professor *Somebody* from the Continent had just let off discoursing on an insufferable new stream of philosophy that nobody understood but about which everybody and his parrot held an opinion. "Any questions?" asked the crank, wiping his bifocals on a monogrammed cravat. Hugo laced his fingers behind his bullish neck with deliberate artlessness. "Jus' one, suh," he drawled in his cadenced patois. "Do you smoke after sex?"

This is the season of my fall. I know it by the way I avoid mirrors, by the dread I wake with. I knew it the first time her lips grazed my cheek, such ready lips. Where are my scruples now? Gone the way of all the righteous words I scrawled into journals, transcribed onto a computer screen, and published in fat hardcover books. The words I hid behind.

It is night. At the Hotel Noir it is always night. Hugo summons Sarah, the soothsayer, to our table on the verandah—they are old friends—and presses a five-dollar bill into her jeweled and sinuous hand.

"What do you wish to know?" asks she.

Hugo warms his snifter over the candle flame, runs the tip of his tongue along his jagged upper lip. He has not shaven and his pirate origins darken every plug of beard. He inclines toward me. "Ask her something, my friend."

As Hugo savors his brandy, I ruminate, though I have

no faith in prophesy and even less in these overly perfumed entrepreneurs who sell it by the quarter hour. My curiosity leans toward the morbid. Already Sarah is fixing me with one of her *eh bien?* looks.

"How it all ends—the final curtain. That we shall wind up at the bottom of the oceans, I need no seer to tell me. The question is, at the very last, who will wield the lightning that thrusts us under, God or man?"

◆

"I am proud to introduce this evening's guest speaker— quiet there in the back, *s'il vous plait!*" Madame Blanc, powdered and anointed from the roots of her faux blonde tresses to her bloated ankles, nudges forward a skinny man in a long-sleeved shirt and Cupper's croquet tie. "The world-renowned archeologist *Docteur* Lyle Clark is on sabbatical from Oxford—"

"Actually," he mumbles, "I'm here conducting research for a study."

Madame flicks open her Chinese fan and waves it with a ferocity that wrests color from the scholar's cheek hollows. "Actually," she says, "I shall let you introduce yourself. You are welcome, of course." Gathering the massive folds of her flowered skirt, she lowers her bulk into an easy chair.

A smattering of applause.

Professor Clark, his gaze averted, thumbs a sheaf of lecture notes. "St. Germaine is a captivating island, an island not only of great natural beauty but one rich in history and culture and… curiosities, if I may use the term." He pauses and his Adam's apple takes an excited little leap. "There is evidence of human habitation on St. Germaine from the Pleistocene epoch. At that time the island had no name and no spoken language. Petroglyphs, however, suggest that the island's earliest inhabitants lived in trees. Recent excavations have yielded artifacts from as far back as the Stone Age, when the sole object of worship appears to have been the dove. Since ancient times, as you may know, the dove has been associated with Venus and pressed into service as a messenger of love. Christians have long considered the dove the one bird into which the devil cannot transform. Recent findings suggest that islanders in the early years A.D. kept enormous aviaries filled with doves—"

"Implausible." Madame's fan slaps the armrest of her chair. "I have not seen a single dove on the whole of the island."

"*Exactement!*" rejoins the scholar in excruciatingly Anglicized French. "In the 17th century, when St. Germaine became patroness of the island, the creatures were virtually annihilated. The islanders built great pyres upon which to incinerate the innocents alive, as evidenced by disinterred hoards of charred bones. At the same time, anyone harboring a dove was considered an idolater and put to death. Missionaries poured into St. Germaine bearing the likeness of the little shepherdess, who was already widely worshipped in the region around Toulouse."

"Such barbarity," utters Hugo, steeling his beast-of-burden shoulders.

Professor Clark concurs with a sigh. "Saint Germaine fared no better than the doves, I'm afraid. Ill from birth, one arm withered, her face covered with oozing sores, she died malnourished in 1601 at the age of twenty-two. When, more than forty years later, laborers accidentally unearthed her body, they found its flesh intact. Today, of course, science would provide an explanation for the phenomenon. Not so in the age of miracles, when the least peculiarity was considered an act of God. The townspeople, overjoyed, laid the body in the parish church, the better to beg favors of it.

And alas, at the height of the French Revolution three zealots snatched the corpse, and in an anticlerical furor that could only be satisfied with blood, dumped it into a trough of quicklime—"

"*Mais non!*"

"*Mais oui,* I regret to say. Nothing remained of the unfortunate Germaine but her bones. To this day they lie in that same parish church encased within a wax effigy—poor likeness, truth be told, but that doesn't seem to trouble the tens of thousands of pilgrims who flock to light candles at her shrine."

The dirge of mineral water going flat in a dozen untouched glasses, each burst bubble mourning the legions of doves, the decomposed saints, upon whose ashes our lives gently teeter. A sun the color of raspberry sorbet melts onto the sills.

Hugo, his tiger eyes alight, swats at a fruit fly. "Why so quiet, my friends? What is history if not one endless assault on love?"

His old flame Clia, elegant in white linen with her slanting cheekbones and queenly bearing, cocks her chin in his direction. "There you go, Fey, spreading sunshine again."

"Can I help it if the world cannot worship what it has not first martyred?"

The professor takes a measured step forward. "Jesus Christ, Mary, the saints from 'a' to zed, Moses, Muhammad, Krishna… and now the environment—polluted oceans, forests scarred by clear-cutting, endangered species… Indeed, there is ample support for such a conclusion. I would encourage you, however, to avoid monolithic thinking. Take St. Germaine as a case in point: never has her polyglot, polychrome society been of one piece. This island can only be characterized by her idiosyncrasies. Wave after wave of colonization, miscegenation, ministry, mutiny, the illicit nature of much of her commerce... have created, in a manner of speaking, a collage of micro-cultures, each with its own gods, its own myths, its own ecstasies of spirit—"

Madame Blanc labors to her feet. "My regrets, but we have come to the dinner hour."

If the patrons of the Hotel Noir hold anything in reverence, it is the evening meal. Fresh gardenias and scented candles adorn the crisp white tablecloths. Tuxedoed waiters bow from the waist as they hold out *la carte.* Tonight's special: fresh-trapped octopus en croute with wild sea mushrooms. The sommelier recommends a '52 Haut-Brion. Hugo and I take our usual table on the verandah. The trade winds blow mild this time of year.

My friend is quiet, almost sullen.

"You miss her, don't you?"   No need to speak the prodigal's name.

"She baits me in public. Never a reasoned argument, just this unrelenting indictment."   His fist strikes the table edge and recoils palm open. "I wouldn't mind, but why must she remain so beautiful? Why must meanness wear so fair a face?"

◆

The walk from the Noir to the town of Calabash, not more than a mile, wends through abandoned cane fields and manure-spattered donkey paths before the two-lane blacktop takes over. Between noon and 3 p.m. the asphalt bubbles like lava. At dusk every roadside lookout fills with tourists, waiting with cocked cameras to capture the ultimate sunset. There is never a good time to make the walk, but I mind it least after dark, by starlight, when lovers huddle in the shadows and every door stands open to the evening breeze.

Tonight I follow the southern branching of the road

past the lime green façade of the *Theatre du Bouffon*, past the whitewashed war memorial with its miniature cannon, past the shave-ice, coconut and comic book venders… until my sights fix on a red and white striped awning: Clia's Odds and Ends.

Once each winter I make a point of sending postcards to my friends and relations up north, mostly to gloat, but also to let them know I have not gone native and that, come April, I will again pack a suitcase and resume my stolid Yankee existence in the suburbs of Boston, Massachusetts. The cards I select say nothing about my second life on St. Germaine. Year after year the same clichéd motifs: palm-fringed beaches, market scenes, and fishermen casting their nets.

I enter the stationery store through a beaded curtain. From the back room Clia Rackham calls out, "Be right there." A kitten, longhaired and white as talcum, coils about my trouser leg. The wire postcard stand bleats as I turn it (the natives assure me I will eventually grow deaf to the plaint of un-oiled hinges).

My choices made, I drift toward the newsstand hoping to catch up on tabloid headlines before the shop owner can chide me for browsing. *Eight Hundred Pound Woman Trapped in Revolving Door* (news or a metaphor for life?).

"Prime Minister's Wife Paralyzed by Face Lift," Clia reads aloud over my shoulder. She has grown cheeky with me since her break with Hugo.

"Bizarre Mating Practices Discovered in Remote Ant Colonies."

She pads away without deigning to laugh. "I liked you better when you were a crusader—didn't you once address the salon on the myth of a free press?"

"Can't a man lay down his shibboleth?"

"And still be a man? I think not, at least not in the eyes of a woman." She places my postcards in a paper bag, closes the cash drawer, and cranks down the shutters. She takes the kitten in her arms. "Tell Hugo that," she says.

"Must you be so hard on him?"

Her coal-cinder eyes glare at me through a spray of white fur. "I'm not the only one he's let down. Hugo Fey had a vision for these islands, he had supporters."

"He lost the election, Clia."

"He lost *one* election. Man's got no mettle. And then he opens a real estate office, of all things. You don't love a place and sell it off piece by piece." She turns from me, her disdain sharper in profile. "I've got to lock up."

She puts me out and I trudge along the street until it dead-ends, then ascend a step path to a row of identical cottages painted all the colors of the rainbow, each one leaning farther out to sea. At the last I wipe my feet on a hemp mat, turn a key in each of two locks, and cross the threshold into a dim foyer.

"*François?*" a voice drifts out to greet me.

My hand rises on reflex to my collar and undoes the topmost button. Midway to the parlor she, who I shall not name, intercepts me with a skittish glance.

"I be low," she whispers.

Her toffee-colored shoulders quiver; the straps of her chemise slip slowly down them. Stifling a sigh, I take a packet of white powder from my trouser pocket and press it into her palm. Her practiced fingers close around it in a death grip.

"Bless you, François," she says, rising timidly on tiptoe to kiss my cheek. "Bless you, *cherie*, bless you…"

◆

"Have mercy on us, Germaine! We who, unworthy,

kneel before you—beggars, sinners, outcasts from grace. Mercy! Our island bears your sainted name, yet goodness does not reach these shores. You are far from us, Germaine. Your ivory white skin shelters at a kinder longitude. We call to you across the sea, across leagues of cold indifference, our hearts tossed upon the waves like flotsam. Without you we are as the jellyfish that wash up on our beaches, we are as the clams. Mercy, our shepherdess! Hold out your hand to these lambs so far from the fold."

A rustle of skirts.

"Dance, brothers and sisters! That's right. Dance for Germaine, who knew so little joy in life. Ill, mistreated, with nothing but charity in her heart for those who wronged her, even in death evil found her. Pity the pure of heart, for they are as magnets for the demons. Mercy! Dance for the little shepherd girl! Dance!"

Fifty bodies move as one in an airless room. The dancers begin to pant then to moan, their limbs drubbing a rhythm. The preacher speaks in tongues, in rivers of verse. A lit candle catches the edge of a crinoline, ignites a holy fire no one has a mind to extinguish. The young dancer, her face upturned, whirls in a flaming nimbus. Chanting the sainted name of their patroness, the congregation dances in and out of her blaze like moths. They dance with their feet on fire. No one opens a window.

In the morning a constable bludgeons down the door of the tabernacle and finds it heaped with ashes.

◆

There are habits one develops at the Noir, ways of filling the long torpid hours of leisure one buys and then must abide. Each day at sunset, seated in the lantern-lit lounge before an enormous picture window with a view of Shipwreck Cove, I take a cocktail. I will my mind blank and watch the gilded orb melt into a dimming turquoise sea, I watch and sip my martini and suck one of the two olives into my mouth, savoring the salt, letting it whet my appetite for a late drawn-out dinner. It is best to avoid eye contact at such times (my fellow guests have grown overly friendly in recent years, contemptuous of solitude). I have learned to hold myself at obtuse angles. The right book can also help: *Aesop's Fables*, for instance, fends off a wide range of intruders.

But today I carry no book. Some trickster god has planted a magnet for honeymooners in my aura. Twice I have had an Instamatic thrust into my hand—*Can you get that guy shucking coconuts in the background?*

No sooner does my tongue wrestle the second olive than Madame Blanc, rouged beneath a fedora the hue of a maraschino cherry, motions me from my perch at the bar to a deserted corner of the lounge, to a table *a deux*. My ritual interrupted I cast about for my shades and room key. The bartender, his pockets jangling with coin, wipes water spots from the draught spigots.

"You are expecting someone?"

"Later." Hugo seldom puts in an appearance before ten.

"Shall I have the boy bring you another martini?"

"I'll wait."

"Such moderation—admirable, I suppose, but it pains me to see a guest deprive himself of so innocent an indulgence." Madame fingers her freshwater pearls one by one as if to arrive at the sum of her qualms. "Thankless business, the life of a hotelier. Seven days a week, twenty-four hours a day, nights, weekends, Christmas... never a moment's peace. *Voilà*—" She extracts a cell phone from her ruffled sleeve. "One has only to ring me. At all hours, like a common servant I'm expected to reprimand a surly waiter, fetch a Justice of the Peace, exterminate a roach, shoo a prostitute from the lobby, pluck a pubic hair from the bathtub drain… There is no limit to the petty demands, the sniveling, and never a word of gratitude." She tosses her layered chins. "If only all my guests were like you. You are a gentleman, a man of obvious breeding. These others… well, money cannot buy that *je ne sais quoi*, that *noblesse*."

As if to prove her point, a ponytailed man in swimming trunks and a fishnet T-shirt pauses at the threshold to discharge sand from his jockstrap.

"One is at the mercy of the marketplace," I say, hoping to put an end to the litany.

"My husband, I suppose you've heard, suffers from ulcers?"

"I'm sorry—"

"My own malady is not so easily diagnosed. I lie awake nights picturing faces, vaguely familiar most of them, but cannot put a name to a single one. I live in a big house filled with strangers. Any passing lunatic might wring my neck in the dark. What's to stop him? I have seen guests fly into a rage over an eyelash in a bowl of soup. I have seen them overturn tables, smash mirrors, hurl television sets from windows… Sometimes I think people are not meant to travel. Demons steal into their baggage, stalk them at every border." Her nethermost chin sinks onto her bosom, which in turn sinks onto the tabletop. "A certain well-known guidebook alleges that the Noir is haunted."

"The very notion—"

"The only ghost to prowl these halls shall be my own!"

"No time soon, I hope."

Her gaze loses focus, the rims of her pastel gray eyes gleam with fluorescent yellow tears. "I am weary, I tell you. I drag through these rooms as if tugging a live volcano behind me. While others enjoy the ocean air, the *ambience*, the best vintages, I look on in dread and wonder, who will set the fire, who draw the gun? There was a time people came to St. Germaine to get away from it all; now, they have many motives, most too horrid to contemplate."

I can only nod. That the islands in this archipelago bear the taint of drug trading, money laundering, smuggling and associated sins, any biped knows.

"Still, I raise my glass with the rest. When their flashcubes go off my lips upturn in the requisite *cheese*. When disaster finally strikes—as it will, as it must—the world will say, but Madame Blanc was so lighthearted, such a bon vivant, never suspecting the torments I live with day and night." She pauses and her manicured hands plumb the depths of her cleavage. "My fan—where could I have left it?" Her upper lip beads with perspiration. She raises a water glass to her face and, eyes closed, presses it to the pinhole pores. "That's better," she sighs.

For a moment I can hear the lapping of waves against the shore, the island's heartbeat; for a moment time itself belongs to the gulls and the tides. Children race along the beach gathering feathers, vacated crab shells, speckled eggs. I long to kick off my shoes and sink bare feet in the sand.

But Madame Blanc has clamped a hand to my wrist. "You have become like family, *Monsieur* Stein. So many years… What a dashing young man you were when you and Mrs. Stein first visited, the very image of Valentino. You had just published that unreadable book—about American communists?"

"Anarchists."

"Of course. At my age the memory flips things about. But I do remember the stir you caused; not that you were the Noir's only author nor its most famous. In those days literati flocked to St. Germaine—Michener, Roth, that manly woman with the filthy hair. You weren't like the others, somehow… I can't put a finger on it."

Not true. I was exactly like the others: vain, self-deluding, never more than a margin's breadth from despair. Only I hadn't realized it yet. My righteousness kept me sifting through the scrapheap of truth until I had assembled a modest body of work, all of it controversial, laced with cyanide and gall. When critics referred to me as relegated to a fringe or underrated, I joked that I had too many scruples to write a bestseller. I was young—what did I know about scruples?

"And here we are."

I can only shrug.

"You can't be more than—fifty-five?"

"Fifty-four."

"Future enough," she sentences me.

How to tell her that my zeal has run out, that I have finally accepted how little I know—how little I will ever know. The arrogance of placing one's name on the jacket of a book! I want only to hide, to burrow into a dune with my few pitiful pleasures and be forgotten.

"You are in the business of immortality, *Monsieur Stein.*" I glance across the table, across the ocean of its polished surface, and see a woman no larger than the image in a camera lens. "We, on the other hand, my poor husband and I, have no such illusions," she drones in a faraway voice. "Now that our sons have left St. Germaine—well, what has all the sacrifice been for? Once the chain hotels erect their neon signs above our termite-ridden eaves, who will remember the Noir? Her walls will crumble, her foundations give way, and all the legends and laughter that gave her life will fade to black—I know it, I've always known it, and yet, each winter when the planes taxi in and that little hum of possibility comes back to the island, I say, one more season, one more..."

◆

From his first appearance in the lobby of the Hotel Noir the man with the silver ponytail and black Zapata mustache made people uncomfortable. Underdressed at the dinner hour, his blue athletic shorts tight in the crotch, he stood hunched over like a beat-up boxer with elbows on the bar. He drank only orange juice, spoke in street slang, monopolized the porcelain saucer of cocktail peanuts ... in short, broke every unwritten rule of etiquette that distinguishes a Noir regular from the mass of common tourists.

I expected him to vanish in a day or two. Visitors of his ilk don't linger on St. Germaine but hop a Cessna to the larger islands, where the music plays louder and a man might indulge his vices in broad daylight. Yet he surprised me, surprised us all, by paying a month's tariff in advance.

He registered under the name of Barly—Shane W. Barly, in full—and gave his home address as Florence, Arizona. He flaunted a stash of crisp new hundreds. Unlike the other guests, he didn't linger in the lounge until dawn. Fresh as aftershave he would traipse about the breakfast room, until Madame had no choice but to reinstate the morning shift, two deaf-mutes trained in the art of the omelet.

"Look," Hugo felt obliged to point out to me, "mud on his shoes."

It is the rare visitor to St. Germaine who tracks in anything other than sand. Eco-tourism has yet to take hold, though the island's interior—volcanic hills and vast tangled rainforest—boast just the sort of rugged inconvenience coveted by paying adventurers. Tourism promoters blame the lag on a lack of infrastructure; too facile an excuse, and not entirely accurate besides. St. Germaine's epic romance with the bulldozer has left her with one of the best road systems south of the Tropic of Capricorn: ring roads and toll roads and scenic routes to nowhere...

If the man with the silver ponytail has been down these routes, no doubt he has trod them by foot. The tropical sun has broiled him raw, except for the portions spared by his blue shorts and laced high-tops. As he stands at the bar downing his nightcap of orange juice in one continuous torrent, I detect the scent of burn ointment.

"Working on your tan?"

He chortles in pain. "Good one, bud."

I retreat behind a week-old *Herald Tribune* and scan the Dow. Another bear market. If the hoped-for upswing doesn't find an axis soon, this time next year I will be watching the snow fall from the double-paned window of my townhouse—like that winter twenty years ago when Sophie got a bewildered expression on her face and folded onto her pregnant belly, forehead softly thumping against the dash-board. "*Oh dear,*" was all she said, all she had time to say, as I leaned on the car horn with the deadweight of my despair.

The blind soothsayer taps her way along the bar trailing the cloying perfume of secrets. "Is that you, my *petit blanc?*" she says in an unplaceable, if decidedly francophone, accent and palpates my wingtips with her cane.

I draw back from her probe.

"And your friend?"

"Hugo is late tonight."

Her blank eyes rest for a moment on my face. "You are always waiting. If you have lost something, waiting will not bring it back. If you are hoping for redemption, waiting will ensure you never earn it. As for Hugo, you waste your time.

He has other things on his mind this night."

When I do not reach for my billfold, she pinches tight her painted lips and begins to tap past me. "One moment," I say and place a pair of tens in her palm. Her advice may vex me, but the poor woman is only trying to earn a livelihood, after all.

The soothsayer pockets the cash and backhands my shin with her cane. "Sightless Sarah needs no one's pity." She does not see me wince.

Shane W. Barly, yawning openly, drops to his feet. "Doesn't anyone sleep on this island?"

I would like to tell him about the dynamiting, about how, once you reach the interior, the roads don't meet up at the junctures. I would like to warn him that people who move millions of dollars in *ganja* and heroin brook no sightseeing in their fortified fiefdoms, but he is already tracking mud up the lobby staircase. Night cannot hold him. While the first wave of diners makes its way toward the gleaming tables, he turns a key in the door of room number 33 and locks it behind him.

◆

"We gather here today, brothers and sisters, not to mourn our brethren who perished in the holy blaze—blessed be they!—but to celebrate the sanctification of their souls. They have drawn near to Germaine, they dwell at her sainted bosom, as we, who sin and repent and sin again, cannot. Blessed, the departed and their blackened bones! Mourn them not, brothers and sisters."

A woman in a plumed yellow hat and matching pumps muzzles her sobs on the sinew of her husband's neck. As if joined by an invisible wire, the congregation lurches to its feet. Hands strain heavenward, chins follow, hips sway like fronds in a typhoon.

"That's right! Do not burden the little shepherdess with your weeping, she who so readily takes our sorrows to her own heart. Fortunate are we who keep the devil from her island with our faith and our fearlessness. The cleansing fire of her mercy awaits every one of us."

"Take me, Germaine!"

"That's right!"

The preacher lifts aloft the urn of ashes and begins to dance, his stocky legs gaining momentum, his rubber-soled feet stamping. The woman in the yellow hat falls moaning to her knees. The preacher waves the urn above her head. "Forsake us not, Germaine! Send us the spark of deliverance! Mercy!" He removes the lid and thrusts in his hand. Circling the congregation on his truncheon-like legs he scatters the ashes, and the dancers lunge for a fistful and smear their faces.

"Yah took my only daughter, Germaine," moans the unplumed dancer, her proud hat trampled underfoot. "Take me, too."

Her husband stops dancing, wipes the death from his eyes. "Stand up, wumman!"

But she hears only the stamping feet.

"Stand up, Mamie! Stand up! Tain yah time yet."

As the dancers close in, the woman limps forward on her belly, licking streaks and swirls of ash from the parish floor.

◆

This is the season of my fall.

For the past dozen-plus winters I have kept a pact with myself: to make love to no woman too poor or dependent to tell me to go to hell. Which, in effect, precludes liaisons with all but a rare few women: peers. Not that I always behave well with these chosen consorts—since my widowing, tenderness comes only in moments—but I refuse to exploit them. I do not take. How, then, to explain my visits to the sylph-limbed girl in the leaning house above the precipice?

My nameless one… washed up orphaned on these shores from a far-flung island where men still carry machetes and women wrap their heads in boldly patterned cloth. She showed me a photograph once.

When I first saw her, a skinny child walking alone with a book clutched to her ribs, she had recently moved in with a grudging relation, an unmarried aunt, whose upgraded hut lay in the fallow cane fields that sprawl to either side of the Noir.

This aunt, noticing my curiosity about the girl, kept close watch. Evenings she would station herself near the fence where her niece sat shucking pigeon peas or sewing the buttons back onto her faded blouses; she would thrust out her hips and eye me with a brazenness that was at once rebuke and invitation. I had the scruples not to bed the woman, who was pretty in a tired way, a chambermaid at one of the less fashionable hotels, and who expected to give herself like ham hocks for any small kindness a man might show her.

Later, when I began making offerings, a handful of bills for her niece's schoolbooks or a bottle of vitamins to build the girl up, she would draw close, reach for the hem of her dress, step out of her plastic shoes. "Let me be nice to yah, suh."

Too easy, too predictable—what other men did.

And maybe she would have preferred it that way, my sweaty white hand on her rump, my groin groping for a hollow, my cum on her mended sheets; *that* she could understand. If only I would take advantage of her poverty, then she need not feel gratitude.

And all the while the girl was growing up, learning loneliness, holding her lips tighter, reading books from other times and places… becoming the enigma that would reveal me to myself. I took notice only at moments, when her eyes would challenge me to or when her turned back would suddenly quiver.

The guardian, spurned, my crisp dollar bills tucked firmly in a fist, stopped inviting me in. "She young, suh, need ripenin'."

But ripen she did not. Last summer, while I kept to my townhouse scribbling notes for a memoir I will never write, the fickle aunt boarded a floatplane for the mainland, leaving the girl a cupboard scantily stocked with canned mackerel, the unpaid gas bill, and a dog-eared Gideon's Bible.

"Men smell when yah starvin', *François.*"

I returned to St. Germaine too late to spare her. No longer a girl, not quite a woman, she bore a terrible knowledge.

"They smell what yah need. They measure it out in thimblefuls—a meal, loose change, the right word. Before yah know, payback time come."

The tracks on her forearms told me the rest.

"Who is he?" I asked.

"Bettah not to know. Next yah be goin' aftah he."

She did not ripen. Her meager flesh clings hard to the bone and her eyes fracture the light. Her mouth, all urgency and tongue, her small sharp breasts an accusation, the needle poised to jab dead-center into the vein… and not yet eighteen. The pimp has left her a black dress, a pair of red high-heels, a shiny purse for her mace gun and her syringes. He has tattooed his insignia, two entwined vipers, onto the rise of her bosom.

"They *smell* what yah need."

I wire my bank for cash, enough to move her to town, enough to support her habit until I figure out what to do next. Every few days I stop by with a book or a bagful of groceries, with the killing white powder, and we sit in the rented sanctuary, in a sunny parlor with a rattan sofa, and dodge each other's eyes.

"He won't come here," I say with sham confidence, "not with the police station so nearby."

"And if he come?" She raises the angle of her chin.

"He won't come."

This is the season of my fear and its denial, of back streets and dank alleys. My sleep churns with the colors of death—the red of cut veins, the black of voids—and the morning light stuns me. I tell no one my dreams.

The nameless one has taken to speaking in the language of Austen and drawing rooms, "proper English," on her lips oddly exotic.

"What is it like to stop at a grand hotel?"

"The Noir? I would hardly call the Noir grand."

"But the chandeliers, the fountains, the limousines pulling up at the door…"

"Most things look better at a distance."

The explanation fails to satisfy. She swivels her torso as if to take aim at me. "Was I a pretty girl, *François*? All those years you visited my aunt, were you thinking, what a lovely, lovely plum?"

I wanted only to relieve a tiny bit of the misery in the world! The child was so bony, so bereft; she had no one. It was not I who discovered the empty fish cans and mangled her innocence—

"Let me be nice to you."

She has been trained to seduce, to wield her body like balm and lightning. A flash of tongue and down go her hands, tracing the curve of waist to hip, hip to pubis, clutching at her sex as if to surrender it whole.

"You don't have to do this." I cut her black dress to pieces with a cuticle scissors and watch her cry over the threads.

"And you don't have to be a holy fool."

I kiss her eyes—the tears sting my tongue—and stagger flint-limbed out into the night before desire or pity can tug me back.

◆

The Noir has always been one of those hostelries designated as a *Hot Spot for Romance*, blessed by Eros with the insinuating light and shadow of a pleasure garden. Honeymooners drift feather-limbed through the lobby trailing the heady fragrance of new desire. Prowling divorcees in deck shoes and false eyelashes line the bar. A man alone might have his pick (even a man cursed with scruples will find it hard to ignore the come-hither looks cast his way).

Tonight it is a sleek, ageless brunette in sarong whose heat wafts toward me, whose eyes follow the movement of the glass to and from my lips. I fix my gaze on Shipwreck Cove and pretend not to notice her smooth midriff, assertive *mons veneris*, lolling ankles… but the resemblance is not lost on me.

Sophie.

The brunette swivels breathily on the barstool, her slender ankles keeping time with the waves. She ventures one of those sad, muted smiles reminiscent of a Renaissance Madonna.

Sophie.

Beside me in the passenger seat of my '79 Accord. Beside me, so close I might plant a kiss on her undefended neck. The window is open and her spicy, teasing perfume plays on the breeze.

She gazes toward me, strokes my cheek. "One day we'll tell our grandchildren about this night. Are you happy?"

Refusing to trivialize my contentment with words, I nuzzle her palm.

"I've thought of a name for the baby."

"Didn't we agree on Mozart Fettuccine Alfredo?"

She laughs, a cut-short laugh. Her hand jerks across the console, lands splay-fingered between her eyes.

"Headache?"

"Oh dear..."

I glance sideways. Her torso curls forward to meet her belly; her forehead thumps against the dashboard; her tender eyes swerve toward me.

"Drive carefully, darling."

My foot hits the brake, the car skids, spins, and it is over—my happiness, our future.

I will not trouble the brunette with the story, though her sighs dare me to unravel her filmy sarong. The small, lovely mystery of her body will remain intact. She will forget me—perhaps, already has.

The sun sets, stranding the lonely in their longing. Night at the Hotel Noir.

◆

Hugo rings me from the lobby.

"Throw some clothes on. I've come to kidnap your sorry carcass."

"In broad daylight?" My eyes drift to the digital display on the clock radio: 10:15. I toss aside a week-old *Herald Tribune,* step into beach mules, and run a hand through my salt-stiffened hair.

"Stop grousing, man. The ferry leaves in twenty minutes."

A deviation from routine: Hugo's weathered Citroen idling at the doorstep, the radio shrill with *Sing! Blow up the bank and sing...* The mood is vaguely festive, vaguely ominous. My friend drives fast, blows his horn at anything that dares come between the front fender and his whim. He takes a cell phone from the console, marks a local number, and says, "Fey here. Yah hold dat boat, arright?"

Moments later we lurch to a halt at the pier. The ferry, its weary engine chugging, is already inching out to sea. Hugo kills the engine, leaps from the car, and rifles through the trunk. His arms fill with brown paper bags and glossy magazines. He pivots, spots a flower vendor, and buys a bouquet of hibiscus and bird-of-paradise, not waiting for change.

Once onboard, seated on the hard wooden benches with their incised graffiti, I finally ask, "Where the hell are you taking me?"

"Home," he says simply, as if our destination had been obvious all along. His scars, a jagged teardrop down each cheek, turn mauve against the bronze of his complexion. On some faces the cuts might blemish or detract from a given set of features, but on Hugo's face they confer authority. Anyone on these islands can tell you their story.

"Great." I snap on my shades. "Maybe your old pals will slice off an ear this time, or a testicle."

Hugo gazes out over the frothy sea with apparent serenity. "That score's been settled. Drug dealers have the run of the place. New Prime Minister doesn't lift a pinky, so long as they contribute to his campaign and shell out for the occasional fête."

"I don't suppose you're planning a coup?"

The cords on Hugo's neck rise to the surface and pulse. "I don't suppose you're volunteering a testicle of your own to the cause?"

A sloe-eyed woman in a gold lamé miniskirt brushes past him with a wink.

"Catch you later, honey bee," he croons in a low voice. The boat belches a puff of blue-gray smoke and lurches forward. Hugo, the thread of his argument unbroken, sits tall. "I gave my pound of flesh—for what? Location alone dooms us, pinned between the two Americas, between deep pockets and misery. How can you expect people to work cane and bananas with the Yanks willing to pay any price for a fix?"

The boat docks and passengers file off, lugging shopping sacks, balancing pots and boxes atop their heads. Beyond the bustle of the tiny harbor, the dirt roads wind with seeming aimlessness. I make out a church, a dance hall, and little else. Hugo steers me by a shoulder. "Look, my friend, it wasn't any kingpin who carved up my face: some fisherman's son with a couple of acres of *ganja* under cultivation spared his boss the trouble. For the first time in his life he was going to bed every night with a full belly, and he didn't want some upstart reformer diddling with his livelihood."

From the windows and verandahs of the modest clapboard homes we pass, women call out greetings; men tip their straw hats. Hugo smiles, waves to left and right, but every so often he veers, his gaze stalking an invisible enemy.

"It's still home," he says.

I gaze about in wonder. There is a rugged, ragged, brimming-over appeal to the place that distracts from its poverty. Children race by three-to-a-bicycle. "Reminds me of St. Germaine twenty years ago."

"The out islands haven't changed much. Fabula has always been the buck-toothed stepsister—shallow harbors, black sand beaches, no gambling casino. Cruise ships snub her. Nothing to do but fish."

"Is that what your father did?"

We fall out of step, our shadows soundlessly colliding.

"My father, as far as I know, never cast a line. He was a merchant, Venezuelan by birth, with his own fleet. Not someone to put down roots. Came through Fabula for the last time in the early '70s when I was still young enough to want to be like him. Gave my mother an accordion file full of stock certificates and made her promise to send me north to university. I still ask myself how he knew—knew he wouldn't be coming back. Men who love the sea live with death every day. Camille took him down, and I don't doubt he loved her, too."

He waves me through the open gate of a whitewashed cottage. A gaggle of guinea hens waddles toward us, their useless wings drooping. A raisin-faced matron in a nautical-print dress and unmatched kerchief throws open the front door and stands on the threshold wiping her palms on the crisp green fabric of her apron. Hugo gives her a smooch on the withered cheek, presses the bouquet into her arms.

"Quick, inside wit' yah," she scolds, holding a smile in check until she has shepherded us both to the illusive safety of her kitchen. "No tellin' who's about." She draws closed the bright chintz curtains.

"Mama, say hello to my friend Francis."

"I was just headin' dat way, a wumman can only move so fast." She lays a warm crinkled hand on my forearm. "Make like in your own house. Hungry?"

Replies Hugo, "I've been craving your famous rice n' peas."

"Dat so, child? Sit down, but don' be stayin' long." Her brow furrows into a grid of worries. "Yah may be quits from public life, but the public not lettin' yah go so easy. Cousin Cosmo say dey makin' melee 'bout yah at the barber shop."

Hugo nudges me into a chair. "It will pass."

"Yah think?" she says, her uncertainty as plain as the cast iron skillet she wrests from its peg beside the propane stove.

Soon the warmed-over rice begins to sizzle and an aroma at once sweet and pungent rises on the saturated air. Hugo sniffs audibly. "I brought you a few things." He unloads the contents of the brown paper bags item by item. The tabletop fills with kitchen gadgets, porcelain figurines, chocolates, scalloped guest soaps, skeins of embroidery thread, an eyelash curler, and last, the *piece de la resistance*, a felt bowler festooned with silk flowers.

"Yah shouldna go spendin' your money like dat," she chides, casting avid glances at the hat.

"You're my girl."

His mother blushes, switches off the flame beneath the skillet, and heaps two plates with the viscous mixture. "Yah too thin, Francis. Dat fancy touris' food be corrodin' your bones." She pours two glasses of lemonade. "Hurry now, Hugo. Word travel on dis island lika jet plane."

"Like a guided missile," my friend says grimly.

The old woman paces until we have cleaned our plates and then nudges us toward the door. "Call ahead nex' time. I'll chop the head off one of dem hens." As we step onto the verandah, she claps something small and metallic into her son's hand. "Yah take care," she whispers.

Not until we're back on the ferry does Hugo open his fist, revealing a tarnished medal on a gold chain. "Saint Christopher," he says bitterly. "It belonged to my father."

The engine rumbles to life and the ferry huffs toward open sea. A companionable silence falls over the passengers.

Hugo sits hunched in his seat gazing back toward Fabula through half-closed lids.

We are midway to St. Germaine when he sits up and murmurs, "Thank you, Francis."

"What for?"

A glint of mirth plays at the corners of his mouth. "For not being one more Jimbo Yank."

◆

The leaning house faces off with a northerly. The front door judders on its hinges. As I let myself in, the nameless one, wrapped in a pale pink towel, darts from the bath to the bedroom and calls, "Won't be a minute."

No less an enigma than the little girl with missing teeth and missing buttons whose solitude I chanced to enter, she leaves no trail. I gaze about the small parlor, searching for clues—an open book, an empty cup—the story of her hours alone in the furnished rental with its ruffled curtains and lampshades and vases of plastic flowers. She keeps the room spotless. The wood smells of lemon oil, the upholstery of drug store cologne.

"Are you looking for something?" She has put on a cotton sundress, a pair of rubber sandals. Her wet hair hangs in ringlets.

"Do you have everything you need?"

She cannot stifle a tart little smile. "There's just one thing I need."

I take a seat, hoping she might too. We are awkward in each other's presence, neither one of us at home.

"Is the house okay?"

"I've never lived anywhere this fine. So many windows." She glances at the drawn net curtains. "People could look in."

"You're quiet. I don't see why anyone would bother

you."

"Of course, why would they?" she says without conviction.

We lapse into silence, I hunched forward in my chair, she shifting her weight from one twitchy foot to the other.

"So, what do we do now?" She takes a tentative step toward me, one hand absently tracing circles on her thigh. "Make conversation? I haven't read enough books. Share a meal? I have no appetite."

"I don't come here to be entertained."

She almost smiles. "Why *do* you come?"

"What would happen if I didn't?"

"That wasn't the question."

"But it is—for me."

She circles away, barely deigning to look at me. "Having sex isn't so bad when I'm high. It makes the time pass, at least."

"That's no life. I've told you."

"Afraid I have a disease?"

I get to my feet, feeling old and righteous and more than a little unsteady. "The drugs. They're twisting things. Couldn't you stop—couldn't you, at least, try?"

Panic turns her the color of embers. She starts toward me, hands rising to cup her temples. "Please don't ask me that. I did try. I have tried." She clutches at the tab of my polo. "Jus don' be askin' me, arright?"

"It's all right. It will be all right. I'll come another time."

She turns away and the delicate blades of her back whisper the name of every mortal sin.

◆

The public library on St. Germaine occupies two poorly lit rear rooms of the municipal building. A clubfooted librarian hobbles about in iron-soled shoes. The stacks smell of rat poison and mildew; almost no one comes here—which suits me. Who would want to be discovered hunched in this corner carrel thumbing this suspect tome?

I turn the pages of a musty pharmacopoeia and see the nameless one's face in every margin: *"Heroin users who inject will feel a euphoric surge or 'rush' as it is often called. Animals will work persistently at pressing a bar for the pleasurable sensations induced by opiates. Monkeys have been known to press 12,800 times for a single dose."*

Pleasure, how little she has known of it. To escape into the pages of a book with the night breeze to drive away the overheated thoughts of day, and now—now the white powder, the fleeting euphoria bursting her veins. She has the delicacy not to shoot-up in front of me, but I have seen the rubber tourniquet, the syringes, the little dabs of blood absorbed by squares of toilet tissue. I have seen her savage surrender each time the high takes hold.

"Heroin use can be fatal. Short-term risks include infections such as HIV/AIDS. The long-term user faces additional dangers such as abscesses, cellulitis, liver disease, pulmonary complications... and overdose."

Then there is her coming-down look: eyes haunted, shoulders curled, and the wanting already creeping back. It must stop. I must stop it—but gently, gently...

I have never been able to abide her suffering. It slayed me to watch her mend the moth holes on her threadbare blouses. When other children taunted her or pulled the book from her ribs, my heart would wrench. A Mother Teresa I have never been, but for this one girl, this fallen plum of a girl—then, now, always—what would I not give?

◆

The fine art of wasting time, a hallmark of the Noir,

each day holds less appeal. A grain of sand has taken up residence in the seat of my pants. I gaze out over Shipwreck Cove, across the sheet-like swath of white sand, a blank page. My mind spews book titles: *Tropical Depression, The Clam Man, Island of Lost Luggage...* To write or not to write? To sleep, perchance to dream—but not here, not with the relentless *clink-clink* of ice cubes striking glass.

"Anutha martini?" Shorty asks for the sake of form.

One has always sufficed. Tonight I leave the second olive afloat in the dregs, a monument to temperance. I drop to my feet stone sober and make my way through the lobby at a brisk clip, though I have no appointment to keep, no work in progress.

A front desk clerk jockeys for my attention. "Mistuh Stern?"

"Stein."

He hands me a stamped and sealed envelope. "Dey misspelled your name, suh."

I thank him, and as I ascend the staircase to my suite absently tear open the envelope's flap. The door to room 33 stands open, I can't help but notice, a wash bucket propped on its threshold. Not a soul in sight. A hummingbird, its wings a blue nimbus, sucks sugar water from a plastic feeder. At the end of the corridor I kick off my moccasins and step inside.

The maid has left the air conditioner on high. I switch it off and open the sliding glass door to the balcony. A salt-stung breeze rustles the curtains. I linger for a moment watching the gulls vanish beneath garlands of spume, then I double back, stretch out on the diagonal across the king-size bed, and without haste unfold the letter.

Stern,

I know who you are. I know where you go on Sundays and what you do there. I know your woman and I know what you done to her. For shame!

You will hear from me again.

Your Conscience

I study the letter minutely, turn it over and over in my hands, in my mind, and wonder, *who?* Who has shadowed me on my rounds? Who has something to gain by tormenting me?

Somewhere on this island, too near for comfort, tracking me, dogging my steps, lurks my *Conscience*. In his— or her—eyes I am a child molester. Humbert Humbert in sunscreen. Ladies and gentlemen of the jury, it was not I who discovered the empty fish cans, not I who tattooed the double viper onto her pubescent bosom. I only buy the white powder and take it to her in the leaning house—and oh yes, I pay the rent. I am not a rich man, ladies and gents. In fact, before the year is out I will need to liquidate a considerable portion of my holdings and tighten the proverbial belt. But then again, good people, I may not live to spend the money. The white powder is not easily come by. To find the tattooed man, I must brave the meanest streets, the darkest alleys.

Why? Because the world is not holy unless we make it so. Because I couldn't walk away from a skinny little girl with a book clutched to her protruding ribs, yea because her ribs protruded. I could count them.

◆

Professor Lyle Clark stands smoking beneath the Noir's front portico, pausing every so often to bring his wristwatch to his eyeglass lens and to glance with ill-dissembled impatience down the long and winding driveway. Once the rains began in earnest, late this season, he finally shed his croquet tie. Today he wears an embroidered *guayabera* tucked into wide-wale corduroy slacks. A Panama hat tops his balding pate and a striped golf umbrella hangs on his bony wrist.

Madame Blanc has snubbed the scholar since his presentation at the salon. He has moved to one of the new efficiency apartments Hugo rents fronting the harbor. Occasionally I catch sight of him on the road leading to the fishing villages: he has bought a secondhand Barracuda from a departing expat and it sputters and backfires as he passes.

"Spare a moment?" I say, meaning to ask about a certain editor at Oxford University Press who had once expressed interest in reprinting my seminal work on the philosophical precursors of modern anarchy. At this remove I have little interest in disseminating my arguments, which I have since questioned, reformulated, discarded, but the extra income a new edition could generate seems suddenly a bonanza, and my reluctance one last blip of misguided pride.

Clark muffles a cough with his knuckles. "Gave up smoking twenty years ago; started in again yesterday. This island... bad for the nerves."

I resign myself to the requisite small talk. "Most people find St. Germaine restful. Catatonia seems to be the chief health risk—aside from intestinal parasites and STDs."

"Most people who visit this island never leave the beach," rejoins the skinny man in a decidedly acid tone. "All they see is sand and flesh."

"There's always the pilgrimage to the rum factory."

The professor stabs the tip of his umbrella into a potted begonia. "Open your eyes!"

Not knowing what to make of the outburst, I withdraw

a discreet distance and pretend to monitor the clouds.

"The natives inhabit an alien milieu of perceptions," he goes on. "The glossy ads that lure us here would have us believe them a happy-go-lucky people weaned on sunshine and calypso. Who would suspect their shadow side, the part of them that feeds on the misfortune of others? Did you know that for a hundred years the islanders' chief source of income was wrecking boats they would then salvage? They intentionally misplaced the buoys. Having descended from the likes of Bluebeard, plunder was in their blood." He halts his tirade long enough to drag a folded linen handkerchief across his brow. "The present is no less troubling. One would hardly expect such a history to favorably impact the national character."

"I've always liked the islanders myself. Are you suggesting they should have stayed in their treetops?"

"You say that flippantly, but think. The indigenous tribes of these islands once lived in awe of winged creatures and their freedom, yet how readily they embraced the white man's deities, his gospel of fear and shame. *This,*" he intones, gesturing vaguely toward the hotel, its uniformed staff listless, leaning toward shade, its façade the color of smoked salmon, its marquee touting Happy Hour and in-room movies, "this is the result."

I cannot resist the urge to goad, "Come now, professor, surely there are worse things than Christianity."

"Yes, and you will find them all on St. Germaine."

"That study of yours?"

"I have abandoned it."

Distracted, he fails for a moment to notice the taxi that has pulled up to the Noir and the portly man in Bermuda shorts and high white socks who alights from it.

"Rock fever, Clark?" chides the new arrival, fumbling

in his pockets for change.

He pays the driver, counts his suitcases.

The two men signal in unison for a bellman.

Says the professor amiably, "You'll hate the place, Hedrick.

The portly man, softly wheezing, bends over and hitches up his socks. "I already do."

♦

The photograph is small, blurred, buried on page five of a local tabloid between a story about the smuggling of undocumented Chinese to Miami and an ad for hair pomade.

What draws attention is a single in-focus object: a yellow hat with a long matching plume, mangled almost beyond recognition. The caption reads, *Orgiastic Religious Ritual Claims Another Victim: What Became of Mamie Truelove?*

No article accompanies the photograph, only a second, smaller photograph in black and white: Mamie Truelove as she might have appeared on a driver's license or credit card, an ordinary middle-aged mulatto, hair corn-rowed, face glossy from humidity. Ordinary—which on these islands means burdened, grasping at faith, someone who might never have had her photograph in a newspaper if not for her untimely death and the mystery she poses.

I have seen hundreds of such women clustered on the church steps of a Sunday, chatting beneath hat brims, daubing sweat from their lips with embroidered handkerchiefs. They, not their men, are the backbone of Saint Germaine. Their hands receive the newborn and lay the dead to rest. Their hoarded pennies buy the schoolbooks, pay the grocer, and send the children to bigger islands from which they never return.

What became of Mamie Truelove? Her trampled body suggests an end too terrible to contemplate—why, then, that look of tender submission on her face?

◆

What draws me back to the house of the wicked aunt, who can say, but one late afternoon while the patrons of the Noir roll out of bed and take their first cocktails, I dab sunscreen on my nose and drift to the fallow cane fields. The hut is still standing, but vandals have carried off its one glass windowpane, the propane tank, and the resin Cupid that once held up a birdbath. The door is not locked—the lock, too, has been stolen.

Queasy, I linger on the tiny porch and watch a feral cat sink its teeth into the blown remains of a bunless chilidog. The place has a bad smell. Stopping short of its threshold, I nudge open the door and peer in. Whatever has been spared lies strewn across the floor: hairpins, squeeze bottles of mayonnaise and catsup, sanitary napkins, spoons, forks, the Gideon's Bible that could not preserve innocence. And then I see the graffiti, scrawled across the walls in what appears to be crayon: *Pussy Cheap; Bunny Holes our Specialty; Dick Cheney Ate Here...*

With a crowbar I might demolish the hut plank by plank, with a match and gas can I might torch it. It has never been a home.

I slam shut the door and turn to go. A scrappy teenager with chipped teeth and piercings has positioned himself in my path. Veiling his gaze he waits until I have passed and then whispers at my back, "Mistuh, yah be wantin' a wumman?"

What can I say to make him understand? The nameless one had been young once, had trusted. I stood on this very spot and watched her turn a cartwheel in the sand.

The boy twitches as I veer and then squares his stance. Another year or two and he will harden into manhood; chance will never again catch him off guard.

"Paint the inside of that house for me?"

"Arright," he says uncertainly.

"White. Paint it white."

◆

At first, and for as long as it takes to denude the hors d'oeuvres tray of smoked oysters, no one knows who has invited the ponytailed man to the salon. Attendance has always been strictly controlled by Madame Blanc with preference given to the pedigreed and credentialed. Occasionally, a longtime guest of the salon might bring along a friend, but the ponytailed man is no one's friend, as far as we know. To Madame's chagrin he arrives early, helps himself to a sparkling water and the garnish from a platter of assorted crudités, and takes a seat near the door. Each new arrival walks past him with a measured nod of the head. As the seats fill and a low din of anticipation fills the parlor, the proprietress taps the man on a shoulder with her fan and whispers loudly enough for those nearby to hear, "This is a private function."

The inscrutable Barly stretches out his racehorse legs; he has put on a pair of close-fitting jeans for the occasion. The water glass rests between his thighs. "Not a problem, ma'am," he says evenly. "I have been issued a *private* summons."

She yanks open her fan and begins to ventilate herself with mincing flicks of the wrist. "By whom, if I might ask?"

"By me."

Clia, icily composed in a classic white pantsuit, air-kisses a half dozen nearby acquaintances before occupying the seat beside Barly. They exchange a smile, a lingering look (not without irony), then turn their attention to the podium, where a woman in a red sequined turban and flowing turquoise robes stands hydrating herself from a silver flask.

At my side Hugo clamps his hands together until the knuckles turn blue. The cords of his bullish neck strain against the starched collar of his dress shirt. "Beauty and brazenness spawn at the same web."

I cannot do more than hold my post, a human wedge between Hugo and the other man.

Madame Blanc glances uneasily from one to the other. Her brow pinched into a ledger of rue, she huffs to the front of the room and commences her introduction. "This evening we lift our sights from the dryly academic and purely mundane to the more lofty realms of the spirit. Miss Lilith Stargazer, a renowned practitioner of psycho-somnolent life navigation, joins us from Ojai, California. Today's topic—" She holds an index card at eye level and shrugs her shoulders. "I have always found my own script utterly illegible. You will forgive me."

Miss Stargazer sets down her flask. "We live in confusion," she intones. "We sabotage and deceive ourselves." She gazes from face to face, in no apparent hurry to get on with the talk. "Fortunately, we are wiser asleep than in the waking state. Every night we tell ourselves stories, a nocturnal collection of fables that reveals our deepest fears and brightest hopes. We call these stories dreams. Our dreams are, at once, personal and epic. All humanity dreams, and their dreams flow across the centuries like a luminous river—but do we look into this clear water and see ourselves reflected? Do we allow our dreams to inform our lives?"

Madame Blanc taps her downturned lower lip. "I'm afraid you've lost me."

"We are lost by choice," Miss Stargazer rejoins with

grim serenity. "We have been lost ever since we embraced logic as the sole legitimate mechanism for navigating through life. The moment our heads leave the pillow we don the straitjacket of rationality. We sever our direct line to higher awareness and switch on the morning news."

Asks the proprietress, "Can you interpret dreams?"

"*Anyone* can interpret dreams; it's a matter of courage."

"Courage?"

"Take the most common dream of all: being chased or attacked. This nightmare doubtless originated in primitive times when the threat of being pursued by wild animals or by deadly enemies was part of daily life. Our battle with the beasts of the night allows us to replay that age-old fight for survival; only, today, we confront the attacker on the battlefield of genetic programming, our mind." She steps out from behind the podium and centers her turban. "Who among us is willing to pause that dream, to freeze it at the height of our terror and look the bogeyman straight in the eye? To ask him, who are you? What do you want from me?"

"There is only one bogeyman," mutters Hugo, "and he is us."

Everyone waits for Clia to disparage Hugo's remark—their sparring has become a regular feature of the salon, and though no one would admit it, a source of wry amusement—but for once she has nothing to say. A smile softens the angularity of her jaw.

"But this is all so… abstract," laments Madame Blanc, slack-jointed with ennui. "Someone tell us a dream."

The audience sinks lower into the upholstery, swirling the ice cubes in their wine spritzers. The timid lid their stares.

"How about you?" says Miss Skygazer, gesturing with

her blunt fingertips toward Clia's longhaired companion.

"Sure, I'll tell you one," says Barly, oddly at ease for someone singled out of a crowd. He drapes an arm over the chair back and launches in without preamble: "Okay, so I'm at a party—younger, maybe eighteen or nineteen—and my old man is there. He's wearing one of those shiny paper party hats; his face is red from boozing; he has a chick tucked under each of his arms. He pulls these women to their feet, both of them, and starts dancing something like the watusi, kind of freeform and spastic. And I think hey, wait a second, you're my *father*. You're not supposed to be dinking around like this. I tap him on the shoulder, but he ignores me. He watusies, he boogaloos… and then I see there's a knife stuck in his stomach. 'Hey, Pop,' I say, 'you're bleeding.'

'Never mind that,' he says, 'it's New Year's Eve. I'm having a blast!'

'Pop, you don't understand, there's a knife in your gut. You're dying.' But he just keeps on dancing, keeps on… until the dance floor is covered with blood and everyone's sloshing around in it singing Auld Lang Syne. The taller of his two chicks straddles the knife hilt and grinds nice and easy.

'Aren't these natives a barrel of monkeys?' says my old man. 'Next year I'll bring the camcorder.'"

The fan drops from Madame's hand. Hugo lurches forward to retrieve it, sending his water glass crashing to the parquet.

The proprietress looks suddenly like a pink balloon, thin-skinned and overly distended. She murmurs, "You will forgive me, but I feel a touch of flu coming on. Seasonal malady. I shall not join you *au table* this evening, but do try the fresh catch of the day—eat, drink, and… Hugo, if you would." She takes his arm and exits with more gravity than grace.

◆

Hugo has been avoiding the Noir. No one I ask has seen him. For nearly a week I quash the urge to phone him. Our friendship has always had an easy spontaneity about it, free of the social pressures geography inflicts so disproportionately upon islanders. Each evening I request a table for two, and he either shows up or he doesn't.

I wait for an overcast day and walk to the harbor, where he maintains a hole-in-the-wall office: one desk, two chairs, a bulletin board thick with Polaroids of island real estate for sale or rent. Since the timeshare market went flat and property values skyrocketed, he has taken to pirating tourists from the more posh hotels and installing them in short-term rentals. He has let go his secretary. A *Back in a Moment* sign hangs perpetually on his door and anyone foolish enough to take it seriously quickly learns a lesson in island time. I don't linger. I round the corner and search for him beneath the blue awning of Yvette's Sweet Temptations. At his accustomed table sits an elderly couple in jungle print beach cover-ups, anxiously scraping the whipped cream from their pineapple tarts.

I contemplate taking a taxi to the stilted clapboard cottage on the outskirts of town where Hugo keeps a change of clothes and a Doberman guard dog, but quickly think better of it. Instead I stop at a payphone, get out his business card, and dial—for the first time—the one number listed.

"You have reached the voice mail of Hugo Fey…"

I trudge back toward the Noir by turns troubled and lethargic, in as foul a mood as I have ever grappled on this isle of glad evasions. Hugo's absence drags along with me like leg irons. As I leave the asphalt and the hotel's red-tiled roof comes into view, a wayward impulse tugs me off the path.

Hugo had once shown me the remains of a nearby cemetery, a wind-whipped place with a few toppled headstones where a man might ponder his mortality without inhaling suntan lotion or being accosted by roving banjo players. I make the detour and find the place even more forlorn, more ravaged, more overgrown with weeds than I remembered it. As I stand in the shadow of a tamarind gazing out over a rising sea, a fast-moving figure moves among the graves, stooping every few feet to sink a spade into the earth. A knapsack covers his back. He wears a baseball cap, beneath which hangs a coil of silver hair. My eyes have only to scan his raw red legs in order to confirm his identity beyond any reasonable doubt.

Retreating farther into the shadows, I watch McCabe—alias Barly—work his spade up and down the rows of graves until, at last, he unearths the apparent object of his pillage: a human skull.

Satisfied, he reaches over a shoulder and drops the trophy into his knapsack, then the spade. He claps dirt from his hands. Tensing in the jaw, his black mustache drawn taut across his lips, he pivots, probing the dark tangle of foliage with a wary eye. I stand dead still. I muster breath. Above my head a spider monkey gorges on ripe mangoes and tosses them half-eaten to the ground.

To my relief the grave robber starts back toward the path at a brisk clip, by all appearances oblivious of my presence. A vulture traces the downward spiral of longing with its barbed black wings. McCabe leaves the clearing. Still rationing breath I step out from my hiding place, lick salt from my lips, and retch.

◆

The man in the Bermuda shorts and long white socks, attired for dinner in a conservative beige suit, sends the maitre d'hotel to invite me to his table. Having no handy excuse, I nod my thanks and cross the dining room with forced bonhomie.

There is a generalized din of conversation and cutlery, for which I am grateful. Silence would only accentuate my anxiety. Out the corner of an eye I watch for McCabe, who for all I know might still be awake tracing the bloodstained trail of his father's ghost. At one of the better tables the sommelier pops the cork on a bottle of Dom Perignon. Quartets of sunburned noses wag over bone china plates. And I wonder, not for the first time, why I am here—in this hotel, on this island—idling among the white tablecloths, the sickeningly sweet perfume of gardenias… trifles, trifles, and none of it bringing me any closer to truth or purpose or—do I ask too much?—a sound night's sleep.

"Free to join me? Jolly good." My dinner companion raises his barrel-shaped posterior from the chair and nods to the place setting opposite him. "Have you ordered?"

It occurs to me that I might still get away, if only I can invent a plausible pretext. "Actually, I—no, I haven't."

"I'm having the conch stew."

"I'll have the same."

The Englishman, Professor Ernest Hedrick, 13th Earl of Painswick, pours me a dim rose' from his bottle. I endure it and order a ravishing Lafitte that plays about the palette like a slow kiss. Before long I begin to feel a manly fondness for Lord Ernest and all his line, such stalwart blokes. I forgive them their colonizing zeal and lust for titles, forgive them even the Boston Massacre.

"You publish with Oxford University Press, don't you?" I venture and recall with a pang my aborted conversation with Clark.

"Solid outfit." He puffs out his Windsor knot. "Little weak on marketing, but then scholarship has never been a numbers game."

"I've been meaning to call Dirk Holstein. Does he still acquire manuscripts for the press?"

"Smirking Dirk, you mean?" Hedrick chuckles at the moniker. "Dirk's still there, all right."

"I'll have to give him a call."

"Yes, do, old boy," he says jovially. "Mention my name."

Business concluded, I allow my concentration to amble. The sommelier refills our glasses. Hedrick, it turns out, shares my capacity for lucid carousing. He is midway through a discourse on the carnal aberrations of some half extinct tribe in the hinterlands of Mali by the time we reach the dregs. "Afraid I can't match your vintage on my per diem, old boy, but how about a sherry?"

I decline the offer and splurge on a second Lafitte, though the Dow has taken another dip and my reserve for small indulgences dried up weeks ago. Hedrick raises his glass and I brace for a toast, but all he says is, "Tad tough this conch, don't you think?"

A waiter in a lemon yellow bowtie and matching cummerbund clears the plates from the table and sweeps the crumbs. Our elbows gravitate to the empty spaces. We loosen our ties.

"Have you seen Clark?" I ask.

"Clark? Shipped home yesterday. These interdisciplinary types haven't the mettle for fieldwork, too easily taken in. I'm still sifting Clark's notes. Hard to say how much is hard data and how much the workings of an unhinged imagination."

"Once you've been here long enough, the two merge somehow."

Hedrick glances toward the soothsayer, who taps

among the tables trailing her fringed shawl and the scent of bitter oranges. "Better to err on the side of skepticism, don't you agree?"

We lumber to our feet, each waving the other ahead, and steer an uncertain course toward the bar. Strangers mill about, shedding inhibitions as the moon skulks across the night sky.

"If academia has taught me anything," the Englishman goes on, "it's that people lie—some outright, others by omission, and the rest through embellishment. There's more truth in a grain of sand than you'll ever hear from man, woman, saint or sage. We classicists would sooner trust a potsherd."

The remark sobers me in a way no amount of black coffee could. I sink into a too-low chair, cradle my chin in a ticklish palm, and know that I will not make that call to Smirking Dirk.

"Let me spot you a nightcap," Hedrick says with unflagging good cheer. "I'm moving to the harbor tomorrow, taking Lyle's old place."

"If you should see Hugo—"

"I don't expect to. Took me a fortnight to track him down; told me to leave the key with the maid when I go. Nice enough chap, but you know how lackadaisical these islanders can be."

◆

November 17, 3 a.m. (give or take)

I dream I am alone on a beach at dusk, alone with the purple sky and last golden streaks of light. My shadow sprawls along the shore as far as the sugar mill.

My wife, Sophie, floats in the shallows, her long blonde hair crowned with mollusks. Even before the first star breaks through the dimming sky, the moist skin of her face reflects the constellations. Dazed with wonder, I drop to my knees, crawl to the water's edge, and wade toward her.

"*Francis,*" she whispers, "*the sea is a cold bed.*"

I raise my arms wide and tug the sun down, down, and wrap it gently about my wife's silver-blue body. I smooth back her sodden hair. A wayward wave lifts her high in the water, thrusts her nakedness at the leering moon, carries her away as if she never were.

"*François, I be low.*"

In her place floats the nameless one, slick with froth, gazing up at me through wide phosphorescent eyes.

"I'm just a man. Please, cover yourself. I can't defend against desire—is that a dove between your legs?"

My breath probes her belly. Her thighs part.

"*Her wings be torn, suh. Can yah make she fly?*"

"I know a way." I tow her gently toward shore and lay her spread-eagle on a shoal. "Close your eyes," I say and glide atop her moonlit flesh.

"*Dat tickle.*"

Our hips find a rhythm, sending us rolling through the surf in a tangle of feathers and flotsam. Her wet mouth swims about my ears. Her buttocks, scratchy with sand, heave against my open palms.

"*She be flyin' now, suh!*"

◆

Breathless with dread, with thoughts too long bottled-up and denied, I make my way toward the leaning house. The street hosts more stray dogs than people, sniffing the gutters, scratching their mangy coats. As I draw near, a police car pulls up to the curb and kills its engine. I stop walking, torn between confession and the urge to run.

A cop with wrecking-ball shoulders and eyes like tacks

glides from the car and says, "You from around here?"

"Yes—no. I'm visiting a friend."

He gazes first in one direction and then the other. "Watch yahself. We got reports a criminal's been cruising this neighborhood. Yah look an easy target."

"I'll keep an eye out. Is that all, officer?"

He drums on his holster. "Tip fah a tip?"

"Of course, have one on me," I say and reach for my wallet. A ten-dollar bill buys me a half nod and the man's brawny sweat-soaked back. Readying my keys I continue on, the precipice never more than a heartbeat away.

"Back so soon?" calls the nameless one.

"Don't be alarmed."

We collide in the corridor and she steps away to study my face.

"I've brought you a book." *Madame Bovary.* "An old French soap opera about—never mind, you decide what it's about."

She snatches it from my hands and hungrily reads the back cover.

"There was a policeman outside." Not wanting to upset her, I feign nonchalance. "Apparently, some undesirable has been seen in the area. You'll keep the doors locked?"

She doesn't take her eyes from the book. "Can you get me a gun?"

"Certainly not."

She looks up with thinly veiled scorn and laughs. "That's what I thought you'd say. You can be so... *comme il faut.*"

"I need to sit down."

She trails me to the parlor, the book still in her hand, her expression unreadable.

"It's time we talk. I know so little about you—about

how you see the world, what you want from life, from the future."

"Not long ago I could have answered you plainly." She rubs a premature furrow from her brow. "Before—before, you know—I wanted to be like the heroines in books, to sleep in a proper bed in a room of my own, to attend balls and have suitors. When I read I can almost feel myself inside the skin of those women, can almost feel… entitled. The future? I no longer expect to have a future."

"You have choices."

She upturns her palms and stares into them. "Do I? What choices did my aunt have? She was poor and cleaned toilets. I'm poor—why would my life be any different, any less demeaning?"

"Because you're smart."

She mocks me with a glance.

"You think a gun would help?"

"Forget it. You were the wrong person to ask."

We sit in silence, avoiding each other's eyes. She kicks off her rubber sandals and pads to the window, standing to one side of it with the curtain bunched in her hand.

"Do you dream?" I hear myself say.

"When I can sleep."

"There are people—indigenous people, mostly—who place great stock in dreams. I've only begun recently to take much notice."

Her eyes widen. "My grandmother used to interpret dreams. People would bring her a dozen eggs or an embroidered doily and she would get down her *Compendium of Willful Delusions* and prescribe the correct antidote."

"What sorts of antidotes?"

"Abstinence, bitter herbs, sleeping on glass shards… whatever it might take to bring dreamers to their senses."

"But surely dreams serve some purpose?" Is that a glimmer of accord in my nameless one's eyes? Has she too had her love affair with the night? "I write mine down. Not that I understand them, but sometimes there seems nowhere else to look. Sometimes things happen that make a man wonder if he knows anything at all."

◆

The item is small, not more than two column inches. Its headline: *Brutal Assault on Icon.* A story best told in pictures, two fuzzy snaps—before and after—accompany the text.

Even before its desecration the icon in question, a garish reproduction of Saint Germaine fashioned of plastic and polyester, had an unseemly look about it, a profanity more suggestive of a five-and-dime store than of a house of worship. The saint's acrylic mouth and laminated eyes held no more piety than one might find on the face of a Barbie doll. Row upon row of candles bordered her shiny skirts.

The assailant had to have smothered a hundred flames in order to snatch the saint from her pedestal—"May he burn the hotter in hell for the prayers he snuffed out," a parishioner is quoted as saying.

Decapitated, naked, the icon lies in tatters on the floor. A severed limb reaches for the sea. A cockroach nests in an empty eye socket. The congregation gathers at the padlocked parish doors to wail and fill their mouths with dirt. Inside, a forensics officer kneels beside the broken shell and finds a single word scrawled in blood: *Seductress.*

◆

When the front desk clerk hands me the second letter addressed to Hotel Guest Stern, I tuck it into my breast pocket and head directly for the lounge. I will my gait steady and yet the ground beneath me seems to swim. Only after a stiff martini do I tear open the envelope's flap and read the crudely penned message:

Stern,

Afraid I'd forgotten about you? No chance of that. I'm your conscience, remember? I am with you always, glued to your brain, reading over your shoulder.

I have seen the syringes at the bottom of the trash bin (the ones she double wraps in tin foil). I have seen her red crazywoman eyes. I know what you done to her—don't deny it. You got the money to manipolate unsuspecting girls. Maybe you think it's your right, but no sir, the youth of this island is not for sale.

As I see it, you have two choices: 1) marry the girl, or 2) put $50.000.00 US at the bottom of the trash next Friday (hundred dollar bills will do nice).

Let's keep this friendly, all right? I would hate to have to snap off those writerly hands of yours, François.

The Equalizer

Ladies and gentlemen of the jury, am I to be hounded and bullied into submission by some faceless keeper of morals? What of due process? Exhibit A: my varsity letter in tennis, earned at the expense of my knee cartilage. Exhibit B: my Phi Beta Kappa pin. Exhibit C: my deceased mother, who would swear on any holy text that I never fought or played hooky from school and always took out the garbage without being told.

Should the proffered evidence fail to convince you of my innocence, ask *her*, the nameless one. Ask her. She can tell you about the anguished margin notes. She can show you the offerings—hardcover, paperback—itemize the edibles— scrambled eggs, warmed-over rice. I cook and survey her ribs, such telling protuberances, bare bones of want.

For the record, ladies, gents, I have made inquiries into rehabilitation: twenty-five days; $30,000.00; no guarantees. There is a clinic near my town. People go in substance abusers and come out chain smokers, yet where else can one buy a last chance at living the straight and narrow? Exhibit D: two plane tickets to Boston, economy class. She will need a passport, a winter coat, dark glasses and high-cuffed gloves. Airborne, she will disappear into the bathroom with her syringe and her tourniquet and emerge like vapor. Her temples will pulse to the rhythm of jet engines. It must stop. I must stop it—but gently, gently.

◆

I am on the terrace savoring a first glass of wine when Hugo claps me lightly on a shoulder, unbuttons his silk blazer, and drops into the seat opposite me.

"You're keeping well," he says.

I signal the sommelier for an extra glass. "Not as well as you, my friend, but then I have a few years on you."

We toast each other's health and sit back letting our thoughts fill the silence, and the silence the space between us. It is a mild night, a starry night; shadows drape the cliffs like black lingerie.

"This island is a lethal love," Hugo murmurs. "I can't leave her. I want to, dammit, and I can't."

"People wondered where you'd gone."

"Caracas. My father had a brother there. I went looking for him. The rich are easy to find; their houses are big and everyone recognizes their name."

I wait for him to go on, but he only cranes his neck.

"No moon tonight."

"What did you want with him, after so many years?"

"A handshake? An *abrazo*? Any token display of familial feeling." His neck cords pulse beneath the knot of a paisley tie, but he does not reach for his collar button. "*Don* Angel Cabrera de la Fuente Fria, his lackeys call him, and he lives up to the title. It took me three days to work my way through the maze of secretaries and bodyguards, to gain *entrée* to the mansion on the hill. He was polite, staunchly polite. He had the maid bring me a cup of coffee. We sat on the balcony. I told him I was thinking of relocating to the mainland. All he said was, 'The economy is not good.' I told him how my father had promised to bring my mother and me back to Caracas, once he moored the business and settled down. *Don* Angel shrugged. *The economy is not good.* I got up to leave—what else could I do? He saw me to the door. 'Look, you weren't his only family,' he said. 'My brother collected wives the way a hull draws barnacles; your mother had to have known that.'" Hugo looks away. "Maybe she knew, but *I* didn't."

A sudden gust sends the tablecloths flapping. At the next table a man in blazer and deck shoes lunges for his yachting cap.

"Shall we go inside?" I suggest.

"I'm free now," Hugo says, as if he's not heard me. "No more illusions about who I am or where I belong."

We drink again in silence, looking out over a rippling sea.

"Have you seen her?"

I make the mistake of speaking her name: "You mean Clia?" Hugo winces. "Not lately," I hasten to say, "she's steering clear of this place."

"That man, McCabe. He's no good, you know."

A shudder passes along the blades of my back.

"A friend of mine checked him out. He has a police record, served eight years in a state penitentiary for selling *ganja*."

"That doesn't mean a whole lot up north. The war on drugs has become profitable business. Economically depressed towns compete tooth and nail for prisons. With mandatory sentencing a small-time marijuana dealer can rot behind bars, if he survives a day."

"Auditioning a new book? Haven't heard you ascend the soapbox in a while."

"No book," I assert more volubly than I had intended.

"Then why the head of steam?"

"An old diehard just needs to vent now and then."

"This is personal, Francis," Hugo chides me. He inclines forward and the starlight ups the voltage in his tiger eyes. "People on this island don't like the young McCabe any better than they liked his old man. They don't like the way he's put the moves on Clia. They don't like his swagger. Tell her that."

I wait for the fury to leave his gaze. "Hugo… you could take her back."

"No," he says, steadying his palms on the table edge. "No, I can't be groveling at her feet like a kicked dog for the rest of my life." He sits tall and princely in his buttoned collar. "*She* must come."

◆

Fathers and sons may at first seem oddly paired, but I have come to believe that at their core resides some defining similarity, usually a flaw, waiting to surface. Brett Foster McCabe and his sinister spawn haunt this island in tandem, their genes, their histories, their motives enjoined in ways not yet clear. Another month and it will be New Year's Eve, an anniversary of sorts. For a brief few days, McCabe's name grazes the lips of those with enough seniority to have known him.

One of the bartenders, Shorty, white-haired now, McCabe's favorite "boy" in the days before the stabbing, has been telling the same story for more than a dozen years. Impossible to say what the mulatto thinks of the murdered American, even as he recalls McCabe's chummy disclosures in moments of drunken self-loathing, drunken grandiosity, drunken benevolence…

"Him moody, dat mahn. Every drink changin' de color of de sky."

I myself met him only once, a year before the end. How unthinkable then that a man so vigorous would succumb to a single knife thrust. McCabe had a room-sized presence; not only was he loud but expansive, lavish with hand gestures. A rib-poker.

"What was it he did for a living? Wasn't he in hardware?"

"Him sellin' tools," Shorty says, wiping down the seasoned mahogany bar with a damp rag. "Lawn mowahs, 'lectric hammahs, chain saws…"

"Big spender?"

Shorty raises his rag toward the ceiling. "De Lord rainin' dollah bills on McCabe, yah know."

McCabe's ponytailed son, eyes darkly lit, glides onto the next stool. The barman reaches on reflex for the carton of reconstituted orange juice.

"Make it a double."

Shorty obliges then, summoned by Monsieur Blanc with his signature double handclap, hastens to the far end of the lounge.

Needing somewhere to park my gaze, I stare into my

martini.

"You would think people who live on an island would mind their own business," says the ponytailed man in a low, if not fully contained, voice. "Irks the hell out of me. Where I come from, you learn in a hurry not to go poking your nose into the next guy's armpit."

"You McCabes have a way of calling attention to yourselves, no offense intended."

He laughs in silent heaves. "None taken, bud. What do you suggest, a smoking jacket and bogus Harvard accent? More phonies in this hotel than flies on a turd."

I can't argue with him.

"Me, I don't need to impress anyone."

"Clearly not."

The ceiling fan whines to a halt and I begin to sweat, to sweat down the sides of my nose onto the lip of my glass.

"Look Francis—that's your name, isn't it?—where I come from, we wouldn't be having this conversation. You'd already have a steel-toed boot up your ass." He licks the orange juice from his mustache with exaggerated gusto.

I need hear no more to know that I'm dealing with a man who's done time, a tested man. Between this realization and the next feeble beat of my heart, I catch a rare glimpse of Monsieur Blanc eying us across the lounge with grim deliberation. Shorty trudges forward balancing a tray of clean tumblers on his sunken shoulder.

"Later," says the young McCabe and saunters away with one hand absently shielding his fly.

◆

December 1, upon waking

My son is not yet born. He polliwogs in a dark, warm womb. His mother, within whose body he takes nourishment, follows his every movement with wonder. Although he nestles deep inside her, he can see her face, hear her voice. She is beautiful, radiant, and already she loves him. A blue crib and swaddling clothes wait in a room prepared especially for him. A life waits.

He has yet to be born, but the world's shape floats in his mind. He senses the moon cycles: day and night, the seasons turning, a far-off tide waxing only to wane once again. It will not be easy to become a man.

"Oh dear…"

Something bursts in her. She had been waiting to burst all her life, this nova of a woman.

"Forgive me, my son, but I can't stay."

She goes still inside, her bubbles evanesce. There is nothing for my son to breathe.

A voice as large as the world whispers, *"Come out of there. There's still time."*

But he has already decided to stay inside, to stay with her, to go where she goes.

"Come out, come out…" I beg, losing myself with each strangled syllable. *"Please?"*

◆

A free-floating lassitude marks tonight's salon. Conspicuous by their absence are Clia and Hugo, not to mention the unsavory other man, whose identity is by now common knowledge. Hedrick provides the one new face at the event, and his plaid Bermuda shorts the sole object of merriment. The guest speaker, being local and female, but not particularly attractive or chic, arouses little interest. Unlike other evenings, people linger at the hors d'oeuvres table, whispering and laughing and licking the grease from their fingers with childlike licentiousness.

Madame Blanc arrives late, complaining of migraine,

and with garrulous ill humor shoos the loiterers to their seats. She plants her bulk at what seems an unnatural distance and begins the accustomed introduction.

"The privileged classes have been characterized—unjustly, *bien sûr*—as frivolous, lacking in social consciousness, especially as regards selected segments of society—the poor, immigrants, religious minorities and the so-called dispossessed." She pauses to adjust the tilt of her hat, upon which roosts a pair of stuffed hens frozen forever in beatitude. "I have long pursued in this salon an ideal of inclusiveness, of open dialogue on the burning issues of our day, even when the opinions aired differ from my own. *Liberte! Egalite! Fraternite!* It is in this spirit that I present tonight's speaker, Erwina Basuto, founder of the Plainspeak Institute and author of *Don' Be Tellin' Me: History Debunked*—I hope I've pronounced that correctly." She turns with a flourish toward the podium. "Ms. Basuto, we are at your mercy."

There is no applause, only indrawn breath.

The speaker tenders her lips to the microphone as if to receive a kiss. "Thank you for your kind invitation. I have, until today, never set foot in the Hotel Noir, which has long had a reputation for pandering to moneyed whites. But, like a prophet in Babylon, I go where duty calls me. What I have to say will offend, as well it should. Look at you: on this side of the room pampered honky imperialists *doin' Dixie*, and on that side the bastard offspring of slave masters and their defenseless concubines, watered-down Africans rolling over for a bone. I have news for you: *Massah day dun!*"

A collective rolling of eyeballs as Ms. Basuto refuels for her next sortie.

"Or is it? Just because the cruise ship operators and land developers and multinationals don't crack a whip at us islanders' backs or brand their initials into our flesh doesn't make us free." She juts her lower lip at a well-heeled mulatto in the front row. "No more than that Rolex on your wrist makes you Bill Gates." The man looks around in indignation, but his acquaintances only sit with heads bent and eyes averted awaiting the next blow. *"Don' be tellin' me* the Europeans brought civilization to these islands. There were no slaves among our indigenous predecessors. It took 'civilization' to create the concept of people as chattel. It took 'civilization' to load five million slaves onto ships and deliver them to these shores. It took 'civilization' to classify racial mix by the 128 parts into which the blood was divided, to devise intricate codes by which to justify the abject subjugation of people of color, to institutionalize beating, mutilation, torture and rape. *Don' be tellin' me* we are a color-blind society. You have only to compare the skin tone of a hotel manager with that of a dishwasher to know that we islanders have internalized racism, that we hide our darker-skinned compatriots in the back of the house so as not to disquiet the tourists."

Madame Blanc, eggshell pale beneath her bird's nest hat, pinces my forearm. "This was Clia's idea, you know. I always suspected she had it in for me, but to humiliate me like this…"

I would like to tell her that we can only be humiliated to the degree that we betray our own conscience, but the line sounds too much like something I once said in a book, and who am I to mete out guilt?

◆

What does it matter how the next letter reaches my jelly hands? When a meteor strikes a planet sending it whirli-gigging into the cosmos in a zillion pieces, do the Fates pause to explain? I am a shadowed man—a shadow of a man.

Beyond panic or pain, I tear open the envelope (such a harmless-looking envelope) and read:

What's a matter, Stern, can't count to 50,000?

Let's cut to the take, like you Yanks say. All the under-age pussy in the world can't turn an old dog back into a pup, but the flesh is weak. I'll make this easy for you: name a figure. What's that honey hive of hers worth to you?

And by the way, I know who you hang with at that rich boy hotel. You see them scars on Hugo's face? Look good, cause I'm fixing to make the two of you twins—unless you cooporate, in which case you can keep your good looks. And the honey hive too. I'm feeling genurous.

It's never too late to repent, but I suggest you act fast. The Lord has a long arm. A man don't want to get caught with his pants down on Judggment Day.

The Reckoner

I reach on reflex for my face and shield a cheek, as if there were any defense against lunacy, for surely that is what's stalking me, a lunatic who pontificates even as he slips a grubby hand into my pocket. Ladies and gentlemen of the jury, I know how this must look, sound, smell, but sometimes a person is overcome by a higher impulse. Sometimes a quite ordinary person feels *called*. Okay, so I have the occasional fantasy—she's a woman, after all, and alluring in her way—but I have not, will not, take advantage of her need. Nor will I give in to the demands of this madman, however deft he may be with a knife.

My weary mind frames replies: *Judge not lest you be judged. Whosoever shall smite thee on thy right cheek, turn to him the other also...* If you're going to blackmail me, Reckoner, at least learn how to spell.

The lights flicker and fade, leaving a hundred paying strangers palpating the walls, calling for candles, wine, a last refrain. *I shot the sheriff, but I didn't shoot the deputy...* A gun she wants, and who am I to preach surrender? It is night. At the Hotel Noir it is always night.

◆

My nameless one is a broken vessel, a storm surge of sighs. She does not look at me directly, yet her eyes miss nothing.

"I worry you," she says.

We both pace. The leaning house crimps us body and spirit, yet we don't dare venture out together—*I don't dare.* There is nothing to divert us but the disjointed snippets of conversation people trail past the open windows: *"She husband nothin' but a face mahn...like a shiver in mi ribs... Armageddon... bungadung."*

I speak her name and she starts. "You need to get well. The way you're living, it's untenable."

"Why do you care? I'm not your kin, not your woman; you don't even want me."

I cannot get enough distance to say, *Of course, I want you.* Too dangerous an admission in so small a space. She would misunderstand, reach for her skirt, feign a passion she has never been privileged to feel—*yes, suh, no, suh, anything you like, suh...* I keep to the far wall. "You're a beautiful girl. You're smart. You deserve a life."

"So do you, *François.*"

A reversal not without its grain of truth. To most observers my beachcombing and scribbles lack the order, the heft, of a fully human existence. "There's more than one measure of a life."

To my relief she sits down, looking for a moment almost at ease.

"Tell me more about your grandmother, the interpreter of dreams."

"The killer, you mean? The killer of dreams." Again the bitter smile. "She didn't use a book—I lied about that part—it was all in her head, the symbols, the cures. Where she learned it, I don't know. Perhaps she dreamed it."

A touch of irony (was it the Flaubert?).

"She died young. They weren't above poisoning one another, the various witches in our township. There wasn't fear enough to support a face reader, a palmist, a bone thrower... someone had to be sacrificed."

"You're joking?"

"I'm surmising."

"Still, I can't help but think there's life in dreams, that our nights of seeming oblivion amount to *something*."

The nameless one gives me a look at once inquisitive and pitying. Her eyes linger on my hands. I thrust my fists deep into the pockets of my khakis and edge toward the door.

"You don't have to go." She takes a step toward me. "My aunt had a name for you. Here comes Mr. Hole-in-the-Heart, she would say. She took your money and made fun of you. She told me not to talk to you, that you were just waiting for me to be old enough, old enough to deflower."

The revelation stabs me less than the word: *deflower*—where had she read it?

"I've hurt your feelings." She takes another step, extends her arm in a gesture of succor, but it's the wrist I see, the inflamed blue-gray veins leading from it, the puncture scars. "I've hurt your feelings and you're thinking, the ingratitude! The ingratitude of these women who live in filth and have nothing to offer but their smelly bodies."

"Don't. Please."

She draws into herself, concave, limbless. "Who did you love, *François*? Who was good enough?"

I would like to shake her, to shake her and say, love isn't about *good enough*. If it were, Sophie would never have chosen me, the least worthy of men, the best loved. Had I known she couldn't stay, I would have written sonnets instead of treatises. I would have bought a guitar.

"Try to eat something."

"Right," she says and hugs her own bones.

◆

December 5, awakened by sirens

I am seated in my editor's office, sipping the flavorless coffee his secretary serves in Styrofoam cups. His cut-the-crap eyes, magnified by bifocals, stalk me above the pocked white rim.

"Bestseller!" he says, jubilant. "Your pregnant wife dies of a brain aneurysm en route to the awards ceremony to honor your magnum opus—which, by the way, sold a measly twenty thousand copies before expiring on the remainders table. Your unborn baby—a son, wasn't it?—suffocates in the womb. And suddenly all your pet causes, all your noble pronouncements don't mean bupkes. You're drifting through the empty rooms tearing your hair—what little time has spared—and asking, why me, Lord? Okay, so you don't buy into the Judeo-Christian paradigm, but agnosticism doesn't immunize a person against heartache. And that's my point: For once, kiddo, you are an item. There's a market for first-person pathos. The memoir is coming back in a big way."

"Don't you find what you're saying just a smidgen despicable?"

He looks bitten. "*Francis, Francis... I'm throwing you a lifeline.*"

I pour my coffee onto the rug—an oriental, vaguely Ottoman—and shrug. "It's all an illusion anyway, life. I can't seem to generate much enthusiasm for it." My feet carry me to the door, but there's no knob to turn, no way out. "If I tell you a secret, will you let me go? My wife's brain made a popping sound when she went: *pfut!*"

"*Now you're talking, Francis. Did she have any last words?*"

"She said, oh dear."

"*Just oh dear?*"

I hurl myself teeth-first against the door, but it holds fast.

"*Well, we can always finesse that a bit...*"

◆

I part the beaded curtain and step into Clia's Odds and Ends, where two elderly men in cabana suits stand turning the postcard rack, making it whine. The white kitten, its coat emanating the flowery-acrid smell of flea bath, leaps from the counter to roll and claw at my feet. Clia steps out from the back room accompanied by a fashionably dressed woman, an islander judging by her high cheekbones and incendiary gaze. "You remember Bat," she says.

Ah yes, *Bat the Basher*. "The journalist—how not to remember?" She had worked for the *Tattler*, a local gossip sheet. For several years we seemed always to attend the same parties, the same fundraisers. She spoke of leaving St. Germaine, as many underemployed young women do, but was slow to get up her nerve. "I heard you had gone to Miami. Working on a Master's degree, weren't you?"

"And you, what was it you were working on?" Her speech has all but lost its native cadence.

Clia steps away to attend her customers, leaving me to fend for myself.

The Americanized islander, bolder for her sojourn north, insists, "Refresh my memory."

For a full five minutes, the time it takes a tidal wave to obliterate a city, I skirt the woman's pointed questions and navigate toward generalities: offshore drilling, virtual reality, the proliferation of T-shirt shops along the harbor. Her gravid hip angles toward me like a life vest—which one of us is drowning?

"Don't be a stranger." Bat slips on a pair of leopard-patterned sunglasses and floats into the afternoon glare.

I exhale.

Clia rips the cord from a stack of tabloids. "*The Star* just came in. Catchy little piece on a rare species of man-eating goldfish."

"Actually, I was hoping we might chat."

Her brow arches and a single stitch mars the symmetry of her face. "If it's about last week's salon…"

"No."

"Wait," she says and takes up her post behind the cash register. The old men pay for their postcards and file out.

I approach the counter with forced nonchalance.

"*Don' be tellin' me* you weren't tickled watching Basuto take potshots at Her Royal Majesty." Clia's grin holds more than a hint of malice.

"I don't like racism any more than you do, but to publicly embarrass a person like that—"

"Spare me the sermon, all right?" She closes the cash drawer, not hard but with an eloquent resonance. "Do you expect me to feel remorse because a bigot lost face? She had it coming."

"Clia, it's not my place to give you advice…"

"What is it, Francis? Why this surfeit of humility?" She sweeps the kitten into her arms and nestles her cheek against the snowy fur.

"Look, I'm concerned about McCabe. All types wash up on St. Germaine."

Her face hardens into myriad angles. "If you're talking about the jail term, I know all about it. He was young. He thought he'd found a way out of the family business. Anyway, that's over now. Lesson learned."

"Doesn't his coming to St. Germaine strike you as odd? What is he doing at the Noir?"

"He's not sure what he's doing here. He came on an impulse. His mother died while he was in prison, his girlfriend left him; he had no place else to go. And besides, sometimes a person needs to go back before he can go forward."

"How does he spend his time?"

"Out and about. He's got old friends from his *ganja* days—a man's entitled to have friends, isn't he?"

"That's not the question."

"Cut the *Magnum P.I.* routine, Francis. A person's got a right to privacy." The kitten wriggles free. Clia places both hands on the counter and squares her stance. "Hugo put you up to this?"

I shrug, choosing to evade rather than lie. "I have my reasons for concern: McCabe's prowling, his secrecy, the things he does."

She glances at her wristwatch. "I'm expecting someone, the devil himself." A tight little laugh spills over her lips. "Why can't you just let me be happy? McCabe hasn't harmed anyone."

"*Yet.*"

"Another prophet of doom," she says with a backward

wave of the hand. "Go home to Madame and her house of mirrors. I don't need anyone's advice. I know McCabe's heart, and I know my own." A torrid breeze sets the door beads swaying, clicking. "Get along now."

◆

The church bells ring with more than the usual ferocity. The sun beats down like molten lead. I skulk along the back streets, my shadow elongated, whip thin, and my footfalls a muzzled cry for help. Where is the tattooed man? I retrace my steps, circle, circle again—*where* is the tattooed man?

My nameless one has not been well, has gone too long without. Black crescents rim her fawn eyes. She shrinks from wee, imaginary monsters—spiders, wasps, rats. She cannot concentrate to read and worries her buttons until they come loose.

I try another street, another alley, the fetid-smelling places where women rest their bosoms on window ledges and ring-tailed cats prowl the dumpsters. The church bells peal. A drunk sprawls cradling his genitals on a spread-open newspaper. No tattooed man. No greedy hand of deliverance. The sun climbs higher.

I trudge, defeated, toward the leaning house and turn my keys in the two locks.

"*François?*" Her voice is shrill, all edge.

I hold out my empty palms.

"Don't do this." Her drawing room English slips away. "Why yah be doin' this?"

"The dealer, I can't find him. I can't find anyone."

She runs fingernails up and down her ribs as if to strum them. "Yah lyin'."

I try to lead her to the sofa, but her nervous bones fight me. "We could read a book together. We could read *Madame*

Bovary or *The House of Mirth*—or something Russian, *Anna Karenina,* unless you'd prefer *Dead Souls?* Get your mind off—"

"Yah lyin'. Why, *François?* Why yah be doin' this?" She drops onto the sofa with her limbs askew.

I crouch beside her. "If only I knew what to do..."

She lays a weightless hand on my shoulder. "Take me to water."

My mind frames objections, yet I hear myself tell her, "Get ready then. We'll go to Rogue's Bay."

Her lips graze my forehead. She races to the bedroom on her doe legs and returns moments later wearing a sunhat, dangling a string bag. I put on my dark glasses, double-lock the door behind us, and we walk stiffly down the step street past the rainbow-painted cottages and dozing dogs toward a taxi stand. Midway, she steadies herself against me.

"Do you want to go back?"

She signals 'no' (her hat brim bobs) then looks straight ahead and continues on with small, calculated steps as if walking a tightrope.

There is only one taxi available: dirty, conspicuously dented, its driver catnapping onto the steering wheel. As we ride through town his hawk eye in the rearview mirror goads me, *I know what you done to that girl.* Our destination, an isolated stretch of beach, the sort of place frequented by lovers who can't afford a room, a bed, brings a smirk to his lips. *I know what you done. I know...*

The taxi leaves the broad asphalt and heads south along the coast on a winding ribbon of road. We reach the first township just as church is letting out. Women in bright-hued hats and their suited, sweating men mill about the church steps, the sidewalks. Drunk on gospel, they step heedless into the street. The taxi lurches to a halt. Down the middle of the road marches a man wedged between the two panels of a sandwich sign: *Beware Killer Saint!*

"Dat mahn," mutters the driver. "One day someone gonna flatten he."

"Who is he?"

"Dat be Edwin Truelove."

"Poor soul," says the nameless one. "His wife and daughter died one after the other, no one knows how. He's come unglued."

"Truelove…" I echo. "Name sounds familiar."

We ride on through the miserable little berg with its frying fish and T-shirt shops, its piety and potholes. I turn in my seat for a last glimpse of Edwin Truelove: He is marching up the church steps; the crowd parts as he passes; another step will plant him on the toes of the black-shirted pastor.

The driver accelerates into a hairpin turn, thrusting me sideways against my companion's yielding flank. Her hand reaches on reflex for my arm—such a vulnerable hand, no larger than a child's.

A long, windswept beach comes into view.

"We'll get out here."

The driver's sunglass lenses track me in the mirror; his foot thumps the brake. I pay hurriedly and lead the nameless one, her hand still clutching my arm, down a worn stone path. Unsteady but smiling, she leans into the breeze, pulls toward the sea.

"I've brought you something to swim in." She hands me a pair of baggy trunks, roughly my size. Sensing my disquiet, she adds, "I found them on the beach where my aunt and I used to live."

The explanation, though plausible, doesn't spare me.

"Why François, you're *jealous*."

Her lips smile and pout at the same time. She lets go

my arm and races ahead, stopping just short of the water's edge. For a scant moment she is the sylph I once watched from a distance, strange and alone, her slender limbs an ode to grace. She steps out of her plastic sandals, out of her skirt, unbuttons and discards her blouse. Clad in a bikini too scanty to have been purchased by her aunt, she glances at me over a shoulder, holds captive for a moment the heart within my heart that has always loved her, and wades into the surf.

◆

December 9, rooster hour

I am walking down an alley—an alley not unlike the one I frequent at church time each Sunday, where the tattooed man keeps one hand on a revolver and with the other takes my money. I move surrounded by armies of stray dogs; they nip; they bark. A woman in hair curlers drifts to her window and calls down, *"If you're looking for Lefty, he hasn't come yet."*

"I have a disappearing woman to feed," I call back. "Her veins are hungry."

"Sugar sometimes works. You just shoot it in."

"But the cane fields haven't been worked in years," I feel obliged to remind her. "Where can I find some?"

She laughs her gold teeth out; they land all around me, tinkling. *"Don't tell me you've never had a white woman?"* She leans out and her breasts flop over the window ledge like overfull sacks. *"The men on this block call me White Sugar. Come on up and I'll give you some."*

The dogs bark; they nip. The tattooed man takes aim from the street corner and shoots them dead.

I kneel among the corpses, the beautiful, dripping dead corpses. "You didn't have to kill them."

"Collateral damage," he says with a shrug and turns the

gun barrel on me.

◆

"Mr. Stern?"

I take the plain white envelope from the front desk attendant's outstretched hand without correcting him and walk away with an inner cringe. Steadying myself against each chair back, I cross the sun-spackled lobby with its potted begonias and ascend the stairs to my room. Once inside, I bolt the door, then unbolt it and hang the *Do Not Disturb* sign on the outer knob.

The room is too cold—once again, the maid has ignored my entreaties and left the air conditioner on high. I flick it off and step out onto the balcony. My thumb burrows under the letter's flap and tears it open.

Time's up, Stern.

I don't see no wedding ring on that girl's finger. I don't see no fat American dollars at the bottom of the trash bin. If I didn't know better, I'd think you was iliterate.

Patience may be a virtue, but don't count on any from me. I'm sick and tired of you rich Yanks thinking you own the Lord's wide world and everyone in it. I'm sick of your arogance. I know what you done to that girl and you're not going to get away with it.

You got one more week to make good: either marry her or come up with the cash (I'm upping the stakes to $100,000.00 US).

Just in case you're thinking of taking this matter to the police, let me set you straight: They got no more fondness for your Jimbo ass than the rest of us gots. You're on your own, Stern, and your hour is fast aproaching.

The Mighty Arm of Justice

Hot and cold and raining down sweat I hang over the railing, contemplating the unbroken blue of sea and sky, the immensity, and feeling—not for the first time—cut adrift. Only the memory of the nameless one's lips against mine, her orphaned fingers clasping my chest, anchors me to anything at all.

Hitching my will to a small fierce hope, I stagger inside, pick up the telephone, and hastily mark a number.

"Island Air, how may we help you?"

"I need to move my departure date up. To January 3rd."

"Your name, sir?"

"Stern—I mean Stein. That's *Stein*."

◆

Christmas in the tropics, a good-natured anomaly, grants license to drink more rum, to turn the music up. Those who can afford new clothes parade them; the rest sit on doorsteps rocking babies, changing tracks on the CD player, waiting for a cake to rise. The atmosphere is homier, less frantic than up north. I needn't tear through Nordstrom's buying overpriced gifts. I needn't invent excuses for the dozens of parties I do not attend. Madame Blanc sets a synthetic silver tree at one end of the lobby, an electric menorah at the other, and goes about her business.

Yet still, there is something about the season that never fails to depress me. Somewhere in the background Jesus wonders at the intemperance of it all. It is a bad time of year to be without family, to think too deeply or long about what drives people to such desperate merrymaking. Were it not for my nameless one, I would ignore the coming weeks altogether, sneak away with my ghosts and a ream of paper. But no, she deserves a proper holiday: the traditional meal, a gift chosen just for her.

A word with Yvette of the sweet temptations clinches the menu. "Yah leave it to me: curried goat, rice 'n peas, accras, then come de knock-out—Yvette's worl' famous black cake." She offers to have it delivered.

"I'll swing by for it."

Is that a smirk on her lips? *I know what you done to that girl.* "Arright," she says. "Jus' be here before noon."

The gift takes more thought. I browse the storefronts where T-shirts and snorkels and rhinestone earrings vie for my attention—too commonplace, things a teenage boy might give his first girlfriend. My melancholy deepens. From a passing Jeep the radio wails, *God bless the children because they can't stop what men do!*

I step off the sidewalk and pivot, aware suddenly of the crowd converging from all directions. *We know what you done.* With the humid air heavy on my chest, I steer a course through the handbags and hair pomade. *God bless the children, God bless the...* I stagger up and down curbs, seeing as if through a kaleidoscope the gaily-wrapped boxes, the paper cones dripping red and green and yellow shave ice. *We know what you done.* I duck under parasols, sidestep my own shadow. *We know...* Where the asphalt ends and the road begins to wind, I exhale, wring the sweat from my collar, and break into a run.

◆

A palpable tension pervades the salon. Hugo has returned, Clia not. Madame Blanc, a brimming cornucopia balanced atop her blonde tresses, weaves mingling among the overstuffed armchairs. An air of apology dims her panache. She has forgotten to rouge her cheeks.

"Ye shall hear wars and rumors of wars!" bellows a sackcloth-suited man at the podium. "The sun shall be darkened and the moon shall not give her light, and the stars shall fall from heaven, and the powers of the heavens shall be shaken."

"Matthew 24," whispers Hugo.

"The heavens shall pass away with a great noise."

"Peter 2."

"We are raised on doom. We learn it in Sunday school, see it on TV. Who shall ever forget the sight of Waco burning or the posthumous testimonies of the Heaven's Gate suicides?"

Madame Blanc, her fan aflutter, taps the man on a shoulder. "*Excusez moi,* but you are in the wrong salon. Today's topic was to have been the life of ants. I commissioned the speaker myself."

The man flicks lint from his wide lapel. "You speak of Professor Groats. He could not make it. Family emergency. He asked me to fill in."

Madame lowers her voice. "But who are you? What ever are you going on about?"

He glares over her shoulder and addresses the audience. "Every place and time has promulgated its own apocalyptic vision. I have collected these visions in my book *Doomsday: Shall We Be Delivered?*" He holds up a glossy paperback mottled with fire and brimstone. "'Come Lord Christ, clothed in all thy wrath and judgment, come with all thy vengeance, come!' The followers of Novatian, third century A.D., prayed for the end but were not delivered. The Millerites, nineteenth century, waited quietly in their homes for Armageddon but were not delivered. In the late 1940s various cults watched the skies for the UFO that would bring Christ back to Earth, but they were not delivered. Nostradamus predicted that the King of Terror would descend from the sky around the year 2000, and descend he has. The millennium has crashed down upon us like a barrage of lightning bolts and still we are not delivered."

Hedrick raises his hand. "The Great Death, we now know, took place some 65,000 years ago, virtually eliminating life on this planet. Most likely caused by an asteroid. Are we to presume, because the dinosaurs were obliterated and have not returned, that *they* have been delivered?"

A flurry of laughter.

"Mock me," intones the speaker, "lay the crown of thorns upon my head, but it is you men of science who today bring doom down upon us. Your bombs, your bio-engineered food, your cloned freaks…"

"But I'm just an archaeologist, old boy."

"Your pesticides, your nerve gas, your nuclear power plants…"

"*Assez!*" rasps Madame Blanc, half rising from her seat only to collapse back into it. "We have heard enough. The end does not concern us here. I am in the business of life. I fill people's stomachs and delight their senses; at the Noir one enjoys the most breathtaking vistas, the finest wines, the sweetest *gateaux*. Outside, the world may be rotting on its foundations, hurtling toward calamity… I am powerless to stop it. I can only provide a sanctuary, an interlude, a self-contained splendor from which no one in his right mind would wish to be delivered."

For a moment the audience sits dumbstruck, then Hugo stands and faces the proprietress. I brace for a rebuttal, for the unblunted truth-telling for which Hugo is known, but he says nothing. Instead, he brings his hands together. He applauds Madame Blanc and soon the other guests— those who, in secret, have derided her hauteur, rejoiced in her humiliation—are on their feet around him, offering up an ovation. Beneath her exuberant hat brim Madame bows her head and weeps.

♦

December 22, 4 a.m.

I am teetering along a white line, down a zigzagging road. Cars to either side of me, sun beating down like scalding tar. I wear a two-paneled sign within which I am sandwiched. A man walks toward me, down the same white line, he too trapped within a slogan. Our shadows merge into a single all-engulfing penumbra.

"Excuse me, can you tell me what my sign says?" I ask him.

"*Dunno.*" He taps his square chin. "*It be Greek ta me.*"

He sidesteps, attempting to pass me.

"Wait! You're Edwin Truelove, aren't you?" I clutch at his shirtsleeve. "We are brothers in tragedy: I too have lost a child, a wife."

"*Bruddahs?*"

"So, I'm white—I can't help that. I didn't choose this skin. And besides, I'm a Jew; Jews aren't white in the same sense Christians are; we were slaves once, too."

"*Yah all look de same ta me.*" He trudges on, pointing to his chest. "*Dis be what I got ta say.*"

"Beware killer saint? But what about justice?"

"*Yah can't win against a saint. Germaine got de Pope behind she.*" He turns from me and begins again to walk. "*Nuthin' ta be done, nowhere ta go. A mahn jus' keep walkin' de line, walkin' de line…*"

Aching and sweaty beneath my sandwich board, I tread on his heels. "In that case, let me go with you."

"*No, mahn.*"

"But—but why should we walk the line alone?"

"*De line be narrow.*"

I get a step ahead of him and walking backwards search his face. Its contours are not so much hard as fixed. His eyes tell the whole truth in cuneiform.

"*Dat be strange,*" he says, slowing his step. "*I can read de sign now. It say, loveless.*"

I plant myself in his path like a road marker. "Just loveless?"

"*Turn 'round,*" he instructs me. "*De back say, place stamp here.*"

"That's better, I suppose."

Truelove's cuneiform eyes scan the roadsides, which in a moment have emptied of life. The sky turns the color of tarnished silver. "*No people left. Dey all be at de bottom of de sea.*"

I shrug and trudge on.

Truelove, faintly wheezing, shadows me. "*Jus' tell me, did yah see any lightning?*"

"You can't take these things literally. Loosen the screws in your head."

He glowers at me, and the ciphers in his eyes leap into flame. "*Then what's this?*" He picks up a burnt lamb, and cradling it, walks on.

◆

Hugo arrives later than usual, at the dessert hour, wearing an expression more peppery then sweet. His silk suit coat looks slept-in. He has not shaven.

"Tough night?"

He inclines across the table. "There's been an attempt on the Prime Minister's life." A yellow fire blazes in his eyes that I've not seen there in years, not since his failed election, not since Clia left his bed.

I ask the logical questions—where, when, who?—but events seldom unfold in intelligible episodes on these islands and Hugo's answers cannot but be vague.

"The pol's are keeping it quiet. The would-be assassin got away. Some sort of grassroots movement seems to be developing. Whether or not its emergence is connected to the attempt, who knows?"

"And?"

"Anything that weakens the administration returns power to the people."

"Power? But it's the army and the drug traffickers who have the guns."

"They can't kill *everyone*—and that's who they'll be up against once the movement pulls together, finds a leader."

"You?"

Hugo winces and his scars turn the color of raw steak. "Let them find new blood, someone younger."

"But you can't be more than forty-five."

"Someone who's never known defeat. That's what it takes, Francis, a blind, lethal faith only a young man can have."

"Revolutionaries rarely mature into statesmen. What St. Germaine needs is vision tempered by experience. Only you can give the people that."

He waves the compliment away as if swatting a fly. I press a brandy on him, but he declines it. "I'm an old diehard, same as you, but I'll give what's asked of me. When the time comes."

The soothsayer, her radar attuned to sea changes of the soul, taps toward him.

"*Eh bien,* Hugo? You are like a hurricane in a bottle tonight."

He reaches on reflex for his billfold. "Tell me more, sugar bird."

A five-dollar bill vanishes beneath the gauze of her

shawl. "The storm is not of your making, yet you are at the eye of it. Keep low. Be as the snake in the grass—take a lesson from your friend, the *petit blanc.*" She points in my direction with her chin. "He too has his reasons for discretion."

Hugo arches an eyebrow.

I shrug. "If people didn't presume, didn't assign motives, we could all live in glass houses." My levity is strained and Hugo senses it. "Okay, so I'm a snake but not a venomous one. Life has its rough patches."

The soothsayer turns her vacant eyes to the sea. "Get *her*—you know who I mean—off the island. Do it quickly."

My friend extends a hand. "Look, mahn, if you need help—"

"And as for you," says the seer, touching her cane to Hugo's instep, "take that brandy and drink it down. Destiny will grab you by the throat soon enough." She taps away, trailing the long, frayed fringes of her black shawl.

Hugo reaches for the snifter. "To your health."

"To yours."

Around us the tables begin to empty, the tide of diners to recede. The maitre d'hotel searches the abandoned glasses for unfinished liquor, pockets his tips, and snuffs out the candles one by one.

Hugo pushes back his chair with grim resolve. "We haven't had this conversation."

◆

The alley whistles with wind. The women sentries with their sandbag breasts have abandoned the windows; feral cats prowl the ledges. At the far end, leaning stiff-necked in a doorway, the tattooed man attends to business, arguing in a whisper with a boy whose chest he repeatedly jabs.

I wait until the boy skulks away and quickly make my

approach, my right hand sweating onto a wad of fifty-dollar bills.

The tattooed man has taught me to economize on words. I hand him the cash, he counts it, and claps the square little packets into the palm of my hand.

He gives the impression that his finger never leaves the trigger of a gun, that he would sooner kill me than proffer a greeting. This day he wears dark glasses, the kind that cast back your reflection in triplicate. I look into my own face and see disjunction, sundered hemispheres weighing their separate doubts. The face of the tattooed man, in contrast, gives nothing away. A rock holds more expression.

As he takes my money, I hear myself blurt, "Get me a passport?"

He raises his shades, the better to stare me down. "Who fah?"

"A young lady."

"She got a birth certificate?"

"Undocumented, not from here."

He motions me into the hallway, which smells of rancid lard, of bad plumbing, and for a moment I panic— what's to stop him from pulling that trigger? Who would think to look for me here? He takes a bandanna from a KLM flight bag and mops his slick forehead. "Nex' Sunday yah bring two snaps an' three thousand dollahs."

"I need it fast."

"Five thousand dollahs."

I know better than to haggle.

Forty-eight hours later he hands me a burgundy-colored passport emblazoned with a gold coat-of-arms encircled in fine script: *Honi soit qui mal y pense.* Evil to those who evil think.

"British," gloats my deliverer. "No one mess wit' de

Queen. I tro' in de driving license fah free."

◆

Hedrick calls, sounding like burnt toast. "I've been deported, old boy, tossed out like a football hooligan. Could do with a bit of company."

He arrives at the Noir in his ill-fitting beige suit, carrying himself with exaggerated dignity, playing the part circumstance has thrust on him.

"Don't have much of an appetite—is it my imagination or are people staring? Never did trust that Clark, and now he's gone and sullied me by association, brought shame and dishonor on the alma mater. All our research wasted, wasted, and the Oxford name an object of scorn." He heaves a sigh. "They confiscated my files, you know."

"*Who* confiscated your files?" I lead him by the arm through the open doorway of the dining room, where a kinder light suffuses his scowl.

"Some lackey calling himself the Minister of Education and Culture gave the order. I resisted, nearly came to blows. It was more a matter of principle than anything else. I had no conclusive evidence of any kind to support Clark's hypotheses. The digs turned-up precious few artifacts."

We sit at a rear table, Hedrick with his back to the door, I watching with mounting unease the arriving diners (any one of whom could be Hedrick's minister, come to entertain his cronies at taxpayer expense).

"But why must you leave?"

"Then you haven't heard? It's all over the newspapers. The dove, old boy. Clark came back to the island on the sly, incognito—I had no idea he was here. They say he smuggled in a white dove, took it out to the hills, and let it loose."

"What was the harm in that?"

"Ask the Minister of Education and Culture." He takes

a folded newspaper clipping from his pocket and quickly scans it. "Here's his quote, *Lyle Clark knew our history and used that knowledge to pique a collective nerve and inflict untold mental anguish on the citizens of this island. Had he staged a bogus Second Coming, he could not have insulted us more.*"

"Next they'll be calling him a terrorist."

"This is no joking matter. Between you and me, I shall be the first to demand Clark's resignation. His behavior was appalling: an academic crossing disciplines, tinkering with the living current of history. It's not done."

I set aside the menu. "Granted he had a messiah complex, granted he botched the job, but doesn't the purity of his intention count for something?"

"Purity? The man flew off his rocker. This island was his undoing." The Englishman, mottled in the cheeks, gulps down a glass of water. "How you've managed to maintain equilibrium year after year, I can't imagine. The heat. The insularity. The ennui…"

"You've forgotten the mosquitoes." The sommelier uncorks an '87 Chateau Rothschild. "I don't come to St. Germaine for her climate or her café society, I come to hide."

Hedrick chortles. "Don't tell me you're a fugitive."

"Nothing as romantic as that; just your everyday misfit."

"Plenty of those around."

A tuxedoed waiter approaches with a silver tray and sets out a first course. The maitre d'hotel straightens a fork. Ever distant, Monsieur Blanc directs from the wings with his ubiquitous double handclap.

"I've no appetite," my companion laments, slathering butter onto a dinner roll. "The local press has hounded me; strangers taunt me on the street. The police chief actually had the nerve to station an armed guard at my door, until that friend of yours—"

"Hugo?"

"Until *Hugo* dispatched him with a few choice words."

I smile, an inappropriate response.

"How that man stays alive is anyone's guess. You'd think they would have carved up the rest of him by now."

Deciding against a toast, I clear my palate with the Rothschild. "So... I suppose you'll be starting a new project?"

"Already in progress: a secular reinterpretation of Stonehenge. My life's work." He occults his chewing behind a raised serviette. "And you?"

Already in progress: saving an under-age island female from a life of addiction and sexual slavery. "My editor's been after me to write a memoir."

"Jolly good. I'll watch for it."

The main course arrives like a reprieve. For a full ten minutes Hedrick limits himself to comments on the texture of island beef, tough by European standards, and the chef's over-reliance on mango chutney. I relax my guard.

"This time tomorrow I'll be halfway across the pond, old boy." Hedrick takes a lingering sip of wine. "Can't say I'll miss this place."

"Rock fever?"

"Every man is an island. I, for one, don't choose to be reminded of it by each lapping wave. What wouldn't I give right now for a dark ale in a noisy pub..."

I walk him through the lobby and out the Noir's front entrance, where a brass-buttoned valet waits to fetch the backfiring Barracuda. Hedrick bucks up sufficiently to say, "Awfully good of you to see me into exile, old boy."

As the Barracuda sputters toward us McCabe struts past, whistling, in his blue athletic shorts. Not missing a note, he acknowledges me with a nod and bounds up the front steps two at a time.

"I'm on my way, then." Hedrick claps me on the back. "A memoir, you said? Always thought one had to be either very rich or very ill-behaved to write autobiographically."

"That or desperate."

Hedrick takes the remark for a joke and chortles into his starched collar. "Ring me up when you're on the Continent." Trailing a black cloud, he vanishes into the twilight of chance meetings.

◆

December 24, just before dawn

The day is overcast and I am walking—almost marching, so purposeful is my stride—toward a massive, windowless building. Soldiers guard the entrance. I walk toward them, neither slowing nor quickening pace. Their young pebble-colored faces barely register my presence.

"Let me through," I say.

"*No one get tru.*"

Refusing to look at me, they raise their bayonets.

I fumble in my trouser pocket for the packet of white powder. "Look, I know you're under orders, but wouldn't you rather be blissed-out? Little dope in the bloodstream and you won't need to bully people in order to feel important. Trust me, man, I've seen what this shit can do."

The soldiers confer in whispers until the one nearest me bares his teeth and snatches the packet from my hand.

"*Jus' don' go tellin' de prime ministah.*"

I walk past them without further resistance, push open a heavy metallic door, and find myself in a vast empty foyer. My chest expands as if to house two hearts. I charge into the first office I see and bring my fist down on the desk edge.

"Freeze!"

A sallow man in an expensive, if tasteless, suit leans forward preening his lapels.

"The dove—where are you holding her?"

"Do you know who you're talking to, paste face? Do you have any idea?"

"Your title doesn't impress me. As far as I'm concerned, you're just one more twisted soul wreaking havoc on the masses—what aftershave is that?"

"It's the smell of power, raw unrestrained power." He plucks the carnation from his lapel and crushes it in his ruddy palm. He stands, more wide than tall, and steps out from behind the desk. *"You Ivy League pen-pushers could do with a whiff of reality. Come. I'm going to show you something."*

I follow him down a long narrow corridor, then another, and another… each one more stifling than the last. As we near the end the sound of cooing drifts softly toward us.

The Prime Minister gestures with a flourish toward a heavy-gauge steel cage. Inside stands a heap of spindly bones thinly wrapped in flesh.

"What happened to her feathers?"

"I had them plucked—how else to make her talk? Do you think Clark was acting alone? It's a global conspiracy. These effete intellectuals and their commie friends never miss a chance to strike at the establishment."

I gaze through the metal bars and see a pair of clipped white wings lying in tatters at the dove's feet.

◆

I fumble with the two locks in a stiff wind. A tropical storm is moving toward St, Germaine, charging the air with static, driving people to angry and unnatural acts. All around me the sound of doors slamming, kicked cats yowling. A stab of lightning rends the cloud above my head. The first drops of rain fall hot, mingling with my sweat. I step hurriedly inside.

"*François?*" A twinge of anxiety in the voice. The nameless one stares at me like an effigy awaiting my words, my volition.

"Something wrong?"

"It's late. I thought you wouldn't come."

I wend past her en route to the kitchen. "Market was crowded today; people shopping for the holidays." I open the small, outdated refrigerator and accommodate my armload of plantains, mangoes and brown-shelled eggs on the already crowded shelves. "Have you eaten?"

"Must you ask?"

I close the door and walk back out to the parlor, where the nameless one sits slouched on the sofa, her reed-thin arms reaching for a book, putting it down again.

"Shall I prepare you something?"

Her gaze drops, traces ellipses on the floorboards. "You're not my servant."

I perch at the opposite end of the sofa, close enough to study her face but beyond reach.

She glances at me over a honey-colored shoulder so vulnerable I long to cradle it. "What *am* I to you? Not your woman. Not your own."

"My own?"

"Everyone has got their own: people like themselves, the ones they walk down the street with in broad daylight."

"Some of us are loners."

"Don't tell me you're alone at that hotel. There's music, dancing, people milling about the lobby at all hours— I've seen the women, rich ones with diamonds up and down their bosoms."

"I haven't taken much notice."

"But you must talk to them, you must be with *someone.*"

I exhale into cupped hands and turn to face her. "I had a wife, a wife I loved very much. There have been other women, but not since…" *You.* "If I can't give my whole heart to a woman, can't look at her, touch her, without making comparisons, it wouldn't be fair to go through the motions, would it?"

"Fair? Men don't think that way."

"The men you've known, the way you've known them…."

"I have discernment." She pronounces the word with care, freshly plucked from a book—*Pride and Prejudice? Emma?* "I know that men choose wives from among their own. The others are simple dalliances. The men don't stay, in the end they go back to their snug little world."

"Those are old books you're reading, books from a time when society dictated an individual's choices. I'm not bound by any book."

"Not even the Bible?"

I can't help but laugh. "The Bible least of all. I have no use for other people's dogma and fairytales." I chance a graceless slide toward her, take her chin in my hand, and lift it. "Every person writes his own book with the example of his life. I'm only trying to do what's right."

You're a holy fool, *François.*"

"Maybe." I take the wallet from my back pocket, unfold it, and hand her the two plane tickets to Boston.

She raises her eyebrows, draws her lips taut. Thus armored she holds the tickets to the light, squints to read the small print, and looks away. "Don' be playin' games wit me."

"It's no game. I want to help you. There are doctors up

north who can make you well."

Tears cling to her lashes. She flicks at them with a twitchy index finger. "Don' be fuckin' wit my head."

I reach out and cup my hand to her shoulder, as if this rack of knuckles could hold off the invisible demons of her addiction. "This isn't you speaking but your wounds."

Her arms rise and coil about her ribs. "What were you thinking all those years, Mr. Hole-in-the-Heart? I was a pretty girl once, wasn't I?"

"A lovely, lovely plum."

She buries her face in the upholstery and her shoulders heave. Beyond the leaning walls a clapper rail shrieks. The nameless one veers, thrusts out her punctured and inflamed wrists level with my eyes. I cannot look away. And, once more, I ask myself, why this girl and not another? Not that the question changes anything. It is too late for revisions.

◆

The sun sets like a dropped egg. The Noir's lobby rumbles with beachgoers en route to their rooms, anxious to wash away the grit of day. I motion Madame Blanc to a vacant corner and watch her worry lines deepen into rifts of dread. Before I can begin my recitation, she blurts, "Is something troubling you?"

"Yes—no. Let's sit, shall we?"

"A surly waiter? An impudent maid? Some petty theft?"

"Nothing like that," I assure her.

She lowers herself into a chair with a sigh and readjusts the tilt of her gossamer bonnet. "I have felt for some time that you are not content with us this season. Be frank."

"I am as enchanted with the Noir as ever, madame, but I must cut short my stay. Urgent business back north. Can't be helped."

Her cheeks fall. "Occupancy has not been good."

"Naturally, I would not expect a refund. I simply wanted to give notice, as a courtesy."

In the time it takes to unfurl her fan, she re-inflates. "Your brother is well, I hope?"

"Everyone is well, thank you."

"You have a new book for us, perhaps?"

"No. Actually, it's Sophie's work I need to get in order, a retrospective."

"I should have known. You have never stinted in propagating your wife's legacy. Bravo, *monsieur!* You must let me know the particulars. I have been meaning to make a trip north myself."

"Of course, the particulars…" I rise by degrees from my seat. "Well then, I've taken enough of your time."

Too late. Her lacquered fingernails flutter up from the armrest and pince me by the wrist. "*Monsieur* Stein, if you would you be so kind, I need a speaker for our year-end salon. It has been ages since you last honored us. Could you possibly…?"

"I've gone stale, I'm afraid."

"*Quel sottise!* Nonsense. A mind like yours only improves with age."

The air fills with pheromones and designer perfume as the first wave of guests sweeps down the spiral staircase for a pre-dinner cocktail. Sightless Sarah, beginning her nightly rounds, awakens a dozing fire-eater with her cane. A salvo of giggles.

Madame proffers a measured nod toward a wasp-waisted ingénue in spandex and then swivels back to me with a sour expression. "Victoria Mal," she whispers from behind a cupped hand, "she writes those new *ethnic* romances."

"Madame Blanc, about that salon—"

"I knew I could count on you, Monsieur Stein."

"But—"

She gets briskly to her feet. "Your choice of topics, of course. That you will dazzle us with your wisdom, I have no doubt." Her eyes flit to the dining room, where the young McCabe stands waiting for the double doors to open. "Snapper tonight," she says, continuing to study McCabe as one might an infestation of termites. "*En papillote*, the preparation favored by my husband. We shall send a bottle of our finest Chablis to your table. *Bon apetit!*"

◆

I take a mental inventory of the nameless one's possessions: one family photograph, two dresses, the aforementioned micro-bikini, a pair of plastic shoes, and an armload of books. She lacks everything. Any trinket would satisfy her. Yet I agonize over what gift to give her, mull and maul each possibility. I rule out the practical, the utilitarian; even poor let her know the heart-skip of the frivolous. My offering must not hint at the teasing reveries she inspires. No, its beauty must gladden pure and simple, free of the tactile insinuation of silk or satin, the glittery promise of diamonds.

The stores are crowded with last-minute shoppers like myself. The spirit of the season does not cheer us. We brush the tinsel from our eyes, the better to scan the shelves in their rummaged disarray. Outside, the tropical storm, gathering force, shimmies the plate glass windows, blows down the cardboard Santa, dusts the asphalt with sand and desiccated algae. The air smells of an oil spill three islands east.

I race from one shop to another, my fingertips palpating the cellophane spires, the velvet hollows—nothing quite right, nothing *her*, and more nothing. From one end of Calabash to the other all the Santas blow away, and still the crowds comb the shelves and display cases for that one redeeming bauble. It begins to thunder. My gaze falls on a sapphire pendant, the gemstone large and clear. I have seen a streak of identical blue in the nameless one's dark eyes, as if the sea had flowed in and left its mark.

Noticing my interest, a sales attendant positions the pendant for easier viewing. I reach on reflex for my wallet. The door to the street swings open, admitting a hot gust of wind. At my back I hear a familiar voice tease, "So, Francis, you *are* made of flesh and blood after all."

Clia. Clia, her hair becomingly disheveled and the inscrutable young McCabe on her arm.

"I was just browsing—"

"You have a sweetheart. Anyone I know?"

I orient myself by degrees toward McCabe. "Ghastly weather, eh?"

"Sure, bud."

"Okay, so don't tell me who she is. You devil, had me fooled with that bookish exterior and all the time you've been prowling like the rest." Clia winks.

"It's not what you think."

"Then why are you blushing, Francis?"

The pair steps past me and drifts whispering to the back of the shop—*we know what you done to that girl.* I pay hurriedly and throw myself into the storm, trusting its fury to carry me where I need to go.

◆

Christmas day. The icon of Germaine has been repaired for the occasion—head cemented on, smile retouched. From a distance the saint looks saintly still, but upon closer examination her brokenness, her crooked pieces, assail the eye. She is no match for the shiny baby Jesus, though her disciples swaddle her in velvet and carry her aloft on a petal-strewn altar.

With a thousand voices chanting in tongues, with cries

of hallelujah! hallelujah! the procession sweeps through the center of town to the missionary church. Jesus and Germaine gaze at each other across the void. The wind goes still. There are only the voices, the singing and the chanting. For the first time I'm able to make out the face of the preacher, white, and to hear his speech, marked by the sort of drawl I have tuned-in when the radio dial goes awry and someone from Mobile or Selma implores me to repent before it's too late. The foreigner ascends a platform erected for the occasion, faces the crowd, and calls out, "Dance, brothers and sisters. Dance for Germaine. Dance!"

Unnoticed on the periphery a bent old woman picks up a stone. Wheezing through the spaces of her missing teeth, she shoves through the crowd. She looks up into the face of the broken and mended Germaine, the dead and deadly Germaine, and her arm rears back—

"Dance for the little shepherd girl!"

The old woman pivots, levels her gaze, and hurls the stone at the frothing mouth of the preacher. Blood pours over the bubbles of spit. Dazed, he takes a few dancing steps backward, sideways, loses his grip on the icon. "Don't let she crash!" Every hand outstretches to break the saint's fall.

A second stone hits the preacher, then a rain of stones. Germaine teeters on her pedestal, rose petals raining down, painted smile askew. A police siren wails.

◆

The cake's flesh is sweet, dark.

"Tastes like the black cake my mother used to make." The nameless one licks her lips shiny. "Only better. We couldn't afford butter."

"Have more."

She takes another forkful. "You'll fatten me up yet, *François*."

I set down my plate and watch her. She savors each morsel, daubs crumbs from the corners of her mouth.

"Why aren't you eating?"

Were I honest, were I fool enough to believe in happy endings, the truth of my growing desire might spill across the table like island molasses. "I'm thinking."

In a moment her mood swings from festive to fretful. "About my going north? You're having second thoughts, aren't you?"

"Not at all."

Her brow arches. "I know about taboos—I'm not speaking now about Victorian England. I am *au courant* on certain issues. On more than one occasion you have left behind the *Tribune*. I know that the racial inequities in your country didn't vanish with the Civil Rights movement."

I would like to reassure her, to take her in my arms. Her sudden formality makes the distance between us unbearable. "You're absolutely right. I won't defend my countrymen. There are people who will judge you by the color of your skin, people whose ignorance will keep them from seeing you at all."

"Even your friends will look askance at us, or are you planning to hide me away? Like here?"

"Is that what you think, that I'm ashamed of you?"

She crosses her arms and gazes at me through narrowed lids.

"I'm a guest on St. Germaine. I abide by prevailing mores—not because I agree with them, but to show respect for the people of this island. If I took you out, they would call you *busy*. Whatever we've managed to salvage of your reputation would be ruined."

She pushes back her chair. "Is it my reputation you're concerned about or your own?"

I follow her through the rooms of the small house, in and out of corners, shadows, shadows, and the walls inching toward us.

"Look, if I were younger—"

"I doubt you were ever young."

"Have you any idea—"

"I doubt you have ever acted on impulse, without stopping to analyze the social cost of your slightest gesture."

"Have you *any* idea how beautiful I find you?"

She faces me squarely, raises a hand as if to slap my cheek. "I don't trust pretty words."

"To your credit."

"And besides, I've decided never to wed."

Mansfield Park? Sense and Sensibility? Her diction grows more mannered by the day. "That's settled then. Now please, let's enjoy the day. Santa and his poor bedraggled reindeer have come a long, long way to bring you something special." I take the small velvet box from out my back pocket. "Merry Christmas."

Her expression wavers between a pout and a smile. She snaps open the box, runs a finger along the gold chain to the blue gemstone, runs the same finger down her neck to the crest of her bosom. "My, my…"

She removes the necklace from its plush nest, lifts it to the light.

"Do you like it?" I step behind her to fasten the clasp. The urge to plant a kiss at the nape of her neck makes me fumble. "Hold still."

As she races skittish to the mirror, I ration breath. In a moment she is back, rising on tiptoe to offer me her lips.

◆

December 26, first light

I drag myself from bed, and with my morning musk emanating from gummy mouth and clammy skin, take upon my back a large Star of David—more ergonomically correct than Christ's cross, but unwieldy nonetheless. Thus burdened, I descend the hotel's spiral staircase, maneuver awkwardly through the lobby, and head toward town. As I reach the abandoned cane fields, the nameless one slides down from a fence balancing a bowl of half-shucked pigeon peas in her arms and pads after me.

"*Yah look old today*," she says, timidly touching the points of the star.

Bent beneath the weight of my penance, I can only shrug.

"*Yah got dat Jew smell.*"

"Wait here." I set down the star and dive off the nearest cliff into the sea. The water, cool and bracing, tempts me to linger, but destiny will not wait. I scrabble back to the cane field and find the nameless one seated at the center of the star, head down, shucking peas. "Go home," I tell her.

"*I got no home, yah know dat.*"

I heft the star up over her head and lower it onto my back. She puts a fresh young pea on the tip of her tongue and waggles it back and forth. Silent, we walk in single file through the field. I point toward a promontory at the far end.

She spits the pea into the palm of her hand and studies it. "*I don' like de high places.*"

I turn to her and the star's shadow engulfs the whole of her small kinetic body, casts it into a separate darkness. "Let us always be ready to die."

◆

When late next morning I shuffle into the lobby en route to the coffee urn, the letter, emanating malice, waits in my mail slot.

Yah pissing me off, Stern.

Just so yah know, I been known to chop people up into little pieces. I mean that literarilly. I'm not talking about some make-believe story like in your books. Real life is what I'm talking about—capital "R", capital "E", and so on…

The way I see it, that girl is ready for the meat grinder.

Save her, save me, save us all—fork over the moolah, mahn! Redeem yahself.

The Mincer
Patron Saint of Last Chances

Enough. Enough. In the name of whatever this human Cuisinart considers holy, enough!

◆

My nameless one is not safe. Somewhere, cruising down these streets in a long black Lincoln or hidden behind a curtain with binoculars trained on her door, on her movements through the tidy rented rooms, the Mincer waits for his moment. That's all it takes to end a life, a moment.

"Get me a gun?"

I step out from the leaning house and hear the two locks click shut behind me. My neck hairs prickle. Having no set destination, I walk, back beaded with sweat, eyes casting about. Who or what am I looking for? Would I know my nemesis even if we stood eye-to-eyeball? Would the stench of his anger give him away?

On the corner, leaning against a half-crumbled wall, a pierced and tattooed adolescent loiters trying to look tougher than he is. I nod a greeting then venture, "Watch that house for me?"

"What it need watchin' fah?" he says, not quite meeting my gaze.

"There's trouble in the neighborhood… some sort of hooligan making trouble." I reach for my wallet; he, high-strung, reaches for his switchblade and flicks it open. "I'll pay you four days in advance, how's that?"

His eyes dart to the bills. "Yah CIA or somethin'?"

"Just a friend."

He swipes the bills from my hand and crams them into the pocket of his worn-thin jeans. "I'll watch the house, mistuh, jus' don' mess wit me, arright?"

Business concluded, I continue on my way that much steadier for having engaged a second pair of eyes.

What was it my patron saint called me? An old dog. An old dog sniffing around a honey hive—*"Get me a gun?"* Ladies and gents of the jury, what is my crime, of what am I guilty? Sentence me and be done with it. Lock me away. Only let her live! Let her read and discover beauty (her own and the world's). Let her know love—pure, unselfish, the kind that comes like grace and makes a soul new, as it once did mine.

The pierced and tattooed boy gives a shrill whistle. Heart hammering, I turn and find him still holding up the same wall.

"Where do I get yah," he calls, "if dat hooligan show up?"

"The Noir. You'll find me at the Noir."

◆

The year-end salon, usually poorly attended, draws a record audience, necessitating the addition of folding chairs. Monsieur Blanc, a distant figure in white *guayabera*, white pants, white shoes, claps his hands and a crate of Burgundy materializes on the buffet table as if conjured.

A swarm of acquaintances buzzes about me: the local intelligentsia, calypsonians, bankers and beauty queens, the shrinking clique of aged snowbirds. The dueling scents of salted cod and cocoa butter, of bay leaf and *Eau Sauvage* collide in midair. I sniff my way toward Hugo.

"What do you have for us today, Francis? A formula for the survival of the planet? A mantra to fend off mutant genes?" He sounds tired. His suit jacket, I notice, has that slept-in look again.

"Half the island must be here."

"Doesn't surprise me. The only man on this island with anything to say, and he shuts up like a clam for two decades. Now comes the pearl."

Madame Blanc presses forward to introduce me, though I have exhorted her to forego the ritual. "I shall not sing the praises of Francis Stein. You know him. He is one of us."

Applause, far more of it than is warranted.

I step up to the podium with my lecture notes, uneasy, as I always am in front of a crowd, but with none of my old fire and chutzpah upon which to draw. In truth, I am afraid—to disappoint, to fail to engage. What, after all, do I really know about these people seated hushed and expectant before me? What can I give them? I feel my palms grow moist.

"Friends," I say. "Friends..."

A hundred eyes fix on me. I step out from behind the podium leaving behind my scribblings, the bulleted 'A's, 'B's and 'C's. Let truth speak through me. Let the words issue from somewhere other than this beleaguered brain.

"We can go to the moon, but we can't reduce the risk of total annihilation, can't stop environmental degradation, the demise of the family, human loneliness... We live splintered lives, cut off from our inner voice, from the spirits of our ancestors, from our own passion. In the midst of our toys and trinkets, our petty triumphs, our supposed wealth, we are loveless, loveless."

Madame Blanc reaches into her lace sleeve for a handkerchief. An elderly man traps a wayward tear with the ivory handle of his cane. And somewhere toward the rear of the audience, small and hidden and glaringly conspicuous, the nameless one displays her punctured veins.

"We would rather go to war than acknowledge the humanity of our opponents, would rather create bogeymen than take on the hard work of peacekeeping and compromise. We quote the Bible when it suits us, but when have you heard a politician exhort his constituents to love thine enemy?"

The nameless one, her crazywoman eyes wide as trenches, brandishes her hypodermic needle like a sword.

"We do not love the planet that nourishes us, that makes our very lives possible. If we did, could we clear-cut forests, build nuclear reactors, drop atomic bombs, produce so much garbage that we defile land, sea and air with it?"

How is it that the audience can't see her? *I* see her: punctured and pleading, ribs crying out to be cradled, lips upturned—does there exist a man who would not have kissed her? A single kiss, ladies and gentlemen of the jury. Hand down your verdict and I'll submit to it gladly, only leave me in peace to savor what little pleasure her toffee mouth could give me.

"We do not love even ourselves. If we did, could we smother ourselves with neckties and imprison ourselves within office blocks day in and day out to crunch numbers or to predict the wiles of the marketplace? Could we resign ourselves to the dread and sadness we feel reading the morning headlines? Could we eat take-out at our desks and sleep alone?"

Let me be nice to yah, suh.

"We console ourselves with small indulgences, over-consume, over-achieve... and still the state of things troubles our sleep, piques our conscience. How long can we close our hearts to the despised and dispossessed? What are our slums, our penitentiaries, and our refugee camps if not a reflection of our own lovelessness?"

Hugo, straight and staunch as the trunk of a baobab, raises both palms. "The church, the state, the media muddle our vision with competing lies. What to love? Who to trust? Our hearts are held hostage."

"Fey's on the campaign trail again," quips Clia, offering up a mock toast with her water glass. No one seconds her.

Into the breach I plunge. "There is a concept in Judaism, *tikkun*, that makes it incumbent upon us as human beings to make the world a little better, to complete and perfect the Creator's work. No messiah, past or present, has been able to do it for us. We have no rational reason to believe that a future messiah will relieve us of the duty. Why not begin it now? For love's sake."

◆

December 30, midnight

No sooner do I close my eyes than Sophie—luminous, dark-edged—comes to me. I wait for her to speak but she only looks at me with the sad half-smile that never failed to slay me.

"Forgive me. Had I known you couldn't stay, I would have built a temple to your fecundity. I would have built bell towers. I would have sowed the desert with forget-me-nots..."

The scent of spice bazaars wafts toward me, quickens my pulse, and Sophie turns, lifts like dust into the ether. Longing awakens me, stays with me through the bare sleepless night.

◆

The telephone rings me awake, too early for brunch, too late for a second sleeping pill. A front desk clerk says uncertainly, "There's a man here say he got business with you, suh."

Not thinking, I respond, "Send him up." Only once I have returned the handset to its cradle does panic spring to my throat. *The Mincer*, I tell myself, and fumble with the door bolt.

He surprises me by knocking, so civil a gesture for one bent on dismemberment.

I glance toward the balcony, which hovers three stories above a concrete terrace, nothing to either side and no way down but to leap.

A voice on the other side of the door says, "Hey mistuh, about dat wumman of yours…"

The voice is loud, not hostile exactly, agitated. I open the door and find my paid watcher standing cross-armed, his cheeks a ticktacktoe of fresh red scratch marks.

"Dat wumman," he repeats to my face, "dat wumman of yours—crazy bitch. Came after my balls wit a meat mallet den she scratch my face. Went fah my eyes like she wanted ta tear dem out my head. Told me ta stay away or her old mahn would saw both my arms off."

"Her *old man*?"

"Dat what she say. Anyway, I ain't goin back dere. Ya can keep yah money—and yah wumman. Bitch."

Before I can frame a response, he curses under his breath and stamps back down the staircase. The hotel, oblivious of my dread, relief, astonishment and return to dread, goes on sleeping.

◆

A cloud overarches the leaning house, casting it into shadow. The flamboyan tree hangs heavy with hornet nests. I insert the first key in the first lock and feel the door jerk open, the nameless one's hand gripping the knob, her eyes daring me to justify myself.

"Have I come at a bad time?"

"You hired that boy to spy on me, didn't you?" She does not ask me in, only scowls and steps away from the door.

"I hired him to *protect* you. There's a difference."

"Is there? I can protect myself."

"Can you?"

"That's what guns are for, François, protection."

I close and lock the door. "Guns are for savages. We are civilized people."

She laughs, clutches her ribs.

"Look, the old year is ending, and with it a terrible chapter in your life."

Her laughter subsiding, she mocks, "You make it sound like a book, like something I can close and put back on the shelf. I'm a drug addict, an addict and a whore. But I've made you blush—how little it takes to raise your color. That delicate complexion of yours, so lily white."

"This has nothing to do with skin tone. It never has."

She bunches her hair in both hands. "Are you staying for a while? Because I'm going to need a little—you know what. Before long."

"I'll leave, then."

"See no evil."

"Please don't talk like that."

"Hear no evil."

"I don't know you when you're… like this."

In an instant she is beside me, crouching child-size on the cool tile floor to hug my knees. "You don't need to know me, François." Tears rim her heartbreak eyes. "Just love me a little. Just a little."

◆

Madame Blanc poses beside the ballroom doors, her beaded evening gown accentuating the annual increase of flesh that has begun to droop rather than curve, her diamond tiara gleaming atop her dyed and spit-curled yellow tresses. She has clamped a manicured hand onto Hugo's sleeve. "Be a dear and bring me a glass of punch. The old year has begun to feel quite dreary."

He, regal in a black tux and red cummerbund, complies with his usual gallantry and I am left alone with the proprietress. The parquet wears an extra coat of wax; waiters squeak by in rubber-soled shoes. I glance down and see my own razor-nicked jaw as if through a fog.

"We shall miss you, *Monsieur* Stein," Madame says in pleading voice. "Who knows what the New Year will bring? My husband and I are thinking of replacing the library with a video arcade or perhaps a meditation center with its own resident yogi… keep up with the times. I would like to think we shall see you again?"

"Of course," I reply without conviction.

"What a pleasure to hear it! Always, always you uplift me." Her smile doesn't quite extend to the corners of her mouth. Hugo returns with a brimming champagne glass, its contents glowing neon pink. "*Merci, mon ange.* Now, go amuse yourselves. No long faces tonight. You are my guests, and I want to see you spit in the eye of Father Time with your merriment. *Allons!*"

As we step through the entryway, Hugo's eyes cast about.

"She hasn't arrived yet, maybe she'll have the sense to stay away."

"Sense? She'll come just to torment me."

We perch at one of the smaller tables. Paper dunce caps, blowers, streamers clutter the place settings. Hugo shunts them aside.

"So, what's this I hear about your flying out mid-season?"

"I've been meaning to tell you."

"When? Your flight leaves day after tomorrow. Were you planning to break the news in skywriting?" He inclines toward me and his neck cords strain the symmetry of his starched collar and silk bowtie. "You're a sphinx, Francis. I thought I knew you. I thought we were friends."

"Never doubt that."

"Friends help each other."

"This was something I had to do alone."

Hugo exhales, drops back into his chair with his tiger eyes burning. "Who is she?"

"No one you would know. I've not—" *Deflowered* her, I nearly say. "We're not lovers."

"Then why the secrecy?"

"Keep your hands clean of this, Hugo. People will make the worst of it." My wingtips have begun to pinch. The first casualty of the evening, a scantily clad crone with blue hair, stumbles against my chair leg running a stocking. I take advantage of the distraction. "See, I'm a magnet for calamity."

And then Clia, ravishing in white sequins and tea roses, appears in the reception area, and beside her, wearing one of those one-size-fits-all gabardine suit jackets the hotel keeps on hand for underdressed diners, the ponytailed McCabe.

"The impudence of that woman!" Hugo wrestles his knuckles. "Her own mother wouldn't know her."

Clia wends her way among the tables, her carriage runway-perfect, baiting. She might easily avoid us—the ballroom is the size of a football field—but instead she glances in our direction, offers a measured nod, and nudges her escort into a seat two tables to our left.

Hugo's scars turn the color of embers.

"We could go someplace else," I suggest.

"We're not going anywhere. What will you have to drink?"

I nurse a first champagne; Hugo downs two. The warm-up band, light on brass, croons mechanically, "*Down the way where the nights are gay and the sun shines daily on the mountaintop…*"

Clia, her lips glossed the color of peonies, whispers laughing into McCabe's ear. He laughs, they laugh together… it seems they will never stop laughing.

"It's all a show," Hugo hisses.

"What do you say we circulate a bit? Blameless Baggins is singing down the road."

"Look at her. She's putting on a show and everyone knows it. The Garden Club has already dropped her."

An unseen hand dims the lights. The dance floor fills with silhouettes grinding, some gracefully, others drunkenly, to a slow, relentless beat. Clia, her hips a grail, draws McCabe toward the music.

Hugo stares into his empty glass.

I scan the darkened room for a familiar face, for any convenient diversion. "Isn't that your *honey bee* over there? Looks like she's free tonight."

My companion waves the remark away like smoke.

"The heart is a mystery, Francis, a vault we will never open."

The lights go dimmer still. McCabe, his silver ponytail a beacon, escorts Clia back to their table and heads at a brisk clip for the ballroom doors. Clia drapes a languid arm across her chair back. With her peony lips parted and minx eyes gleaming, she smiles at no one in particular. Hugo feigns interest in the dancers, the better to watch her as she sits swaying to the music, tapping out a rhythm with the dagger-sharp toe of her slingbacks.

"More bubbly?" he asks.

"Not for me. I've resolved to take on the future sober."

"The Puritan in you. Why not leave austere New England once and for all and make a real home for yourself on St. Germaine? A fresh start."

"I just might do that someday."

"Some day. I've heard that before."

A ripple of unease passes through the crowd. Clia stops swaying, stops tapping, her gaze riveted by the returning McCabe. He has removed the gabardine jacket, has, in fact, stripped to the waist. Bold swaths of war paint crisscross his chest. But the eye is drawn higher, to the crown of his head, to his unbound silver tresses, upon which rests a headdress, a diadem like no other.

"Not funny, Shane," I hear Clia say.

"You're right it's not funny."

The errant McCabe draws himself up and slowly pivots. Grown taller in the space of a moment, arms flailing, laughter pouring from his mouth like nails, he dances away from her in his resplendent headdress. I stare hard into the semi-darkness and make out a skull nested in feathers. Written across its frontal lobe in blood-red ink: Brett Foster McCabe, 1938-'82.

Distance opens about the warrior son. The inner

quadrant of the floor empties as the other dancers gravitate toward the fringes. More amused than alarmed, they turn to gawk for a moment or two before resuming their own veiled dramas. In due course a bouncer approaches, his thick arms stiff with intention.

Hugo detains him with a glance. "Let the mahn be. Can't you see he's got business to settle?"

McCabe pummels his bare chest, whirls until his eyes roll back in his head. A cry breaks from his throat: "*Faa— ther!* Father..."

Clia struggles to her feet, not the Clia I have known but a glimmer of a woman, tremulous and alone. For a moment she leans against the table edge—even in the low light I can see her shoulders quiver—then her gaze arcs toward Hugo, rests on his face like dawn's first stirring.

Hugo rises without haste to his full height and holds out his arm. "Will you excuse me, Francis?"

Eleven-thirty, and I've no reason to linger. I slip out the ballroom's rear exit into the waning hours of a night that has already gone on too long. Dragging my shadow after me, I press toward the open doors of jubilation.

In the streets men strut jangling their pockets, kicking away broken bottles of rum; women in skimpy bright dresses dissemble their drunkenness behind a prow of proverbs; and everywhere the music blaring, *God bless the children, God bless the children because they can't stop what men do...*

A pack of stray dogs tears the gristle from a bone. Fireflies strew puddles of light amid the glass shards and entrails.

I walk in all haste toward Calabash, the old year at my back. Alone and not wanting to be. So little time left...

BAT

Through a practiced combination of calling in favors and greasing palms, I've got my hands on copies of Francis Stein's papers: a recent dream journal with entries dating from November 2002, several spiral notebooks filled with snippets of what, one day, might have been a novel about St. Germaine, and two written but unsent postcards. The competition—by which I mean other journalists—will have to wait months for the *corpus delecti* to be released into the public domain.

I have already begun to piece together a biography of the slain American author, whom I knew socially years ago and whose profile I wrote and sold two or three times to local and regional periodicals. Stein was considered something of a celebrity back then. People had seen his face on the talk shows, though few had read his weighty tomes. He had the sort of presence the media naturally pinned honorifics to (*Socrates of the Nuclear Age* was one of the more repeated).

Unlike others of his ilk too proud or too pedantic to paraphrase, Stein made an ally of the sound byte. Ever tanned and relaxed on camera, he looked as if perpetually stepping off a yacht. No one who did not know him personally would ever have suspected the angst and bloated sense of mission with which he pursued his particular brand of truth.

I liked the man I met more than twenty years ago beside the swimming pool of the Hotel Noir. Lean and unpretentiousness, his nose glossy white with sunscreen, he introduced me to his wife (the ill-fated Sophie I will write about at some length later in these pages) and insisted on ordering me a drink. If he resented my intrusion into his leisure, he did not let it show. "You'll be seeing a lot of us on St. Germaine," he told me, pausing to mark his place in a dog-eared paperback. "The beat agrees with me."

Two decades later this same man, rendered has-been by tragedy, bled to death in the hotel's ballroom, bled to death from a wound no larger than a coin slot.

It had been years since I'd seen Stein with any regularity, we were never close, yet the thought of him trailing blood about the dance floor, staggering, dropping to his knees while hundreds of drunken revelers welcomed in the New Year, chastens me. That a man can die alone in the midst of a throng—what have we come to? Had Stein survived his own death, no doubt he would have written a treatise on it.

I don't claim to have Stein's eloquence, his mental acuity, his eye for thwarted love... I have only these salvaged fragments of his life and the resolve to make them whole.

◆

I arrived at the morgue just as Hugo Fey was leaving it. He looked like something ejected from hell—sleepless, unshaven, and the grief lodged in his scars like freshly applied iodine.

We collided in the doorway. He seemed, for a moment, surprised to see me.

"Clia called me about Stein," I offered in explanation. "Look, Hugo, I know you and Stein were close, this has to be hard on you, but did he ever mention any unsavory connections? You know, like he had fallen in with the wrong people?"

"Since when are you a crime reporter, Bat?" He stifled a sigh. "*Tattler* send you?"

"I'm through with the *Tattler*." The words crystallized into fact even as they left my tongue. The following Monday I would hand in the letter of resignation that would free me to reconstruct, book-length, the life and death of Francis Stein. No more woman's page gossip for this player. "When can we talk?"

He exhaled onto his fingertips, ran them along his brow. "Give me a week," he said and was gone.

The attendant, dozing at his metal desk in a glass cubicle, snorted as I entered but did not rouse.

I stepped into the holding room, which was cold and flooded with fluorescent light. Stein's body still lay on the gurney. I recognized him easily: there was no struggle, no suffering on his features. He might have been napping in the shade.

My eyes fixed on the knife wound; a piece of bloodied gauze covered it. I removed the surgical tape that held the bandage in place and touched the scab. I touched the skin to either side of it. I ran an index finger down his sternum to the front of his pants, which were stiff with blood. Intending to scribble a few notes I took the steno-pad from my purse, but my hands had already started to shake.

We meet again, Francis Stein. No running away this time.

♦

I spent the day after Stein's death salving my nerves with Chopin and reading obituaries. It was a yellow day—bleached sky, blinding sun—and the sea smelled of diesel. The neighbor's dog barked without cease.

Owing to concurrent events deemed more newsworthy by those who make such decisions for the rest of us, Stein's end got short shrift.

On the island people's attention from New Year's day through Three Kings' was riveted by an incident without precedent: a parcel containing a brown recluse spider arrived—sender unknown—at the desk of Prime Minister Dunfey. The spider, discovered by Dunfey's social secretary, had spun a dense web while in captivity (a metaphor not lost on the opposition party, whose verbal sallies grow more vitriolic by the day).

Up north, where heroes are made and broken in a column inch, Stein's obituary occupied whatever space was left after reporters sang the praises of an advice columnist who had been dispensing pap to the lovelorn for fully half a century. The account of his murder ran wedged between lengthier stories about homicidal children and suicide bombers.

In death as in life, lesser talents, more sensational tragedies, relegated him to the margins. The *New York Times* mentioned one or two of his early works and awards, identified him as the husband of a renowned artist, and resurrected a head shot that had to have been twenty years old or more (when Stein's hair had been thick and black and he sported a natty little mustache). The *Boston Globe* was kinder, citing the author's lifelong dedication to such causes as civil liberties, a free press and prison reform, and the two or three lectures he gave at Harvard in the years following Sophie's death.

What about Stein the beachcomber, the daydreamer, the Stein who crammed journals with fantastic musings and macabre dreams... what about the Stein who danced himself to death days before his fifty-fifth birthday and left no memoir? That Stein was ours.

I ran a bath. Immersed to the neck in scalding water, I composed my last item for the *Tattler*:

Some of you knew Francis Stein, others have no doubt heard his name. I am privileged to count myself among his acquaintances, though the sorrow and shame of his murder weigh the heavier on me for it. In his lifetime Stein sought justice for those too hungry or oppressed to attain it for themselves. I now seek justice for Francis Stein. A great man has passed. Mourn him. Convict his murderer!

◆

"Suspects? Half de island suspect." My informant cleans his shades, spits, nudges me deeper into the feathery shadows of palm and bamboo, a far-flung and concealed spot, as the nature of our business demands. Wind tears at the fronds. "If yah be expectin' a conviction, das a whole nutha thing."

"I'm not expecting anything. I'm *asking*."

"You've been away too long, Bat." He mimics my English, flattened by a four-year sojourn on the mainland. "This murder will never be solved—why should it be? People would just get ticked-off. Dumb Yank should have had the sense to get himself to hospital."

"Stein was no dumb Yank."

"Not on paper, maybe."

I have nothing to gain by arguing with my informant, whose time I pay dearly for. You might say we are friends, having grown up in the same neighborhood and attended the same Sunday school, but I have no particular liking for the man, and even less trust. Though he wears a uniform, I cannot say with certainty which side of the law he serves.

"Man gets stabbed with a *kitchen* knife—any bitch can carve a ham might have done it. It didn't happen at his hotel either: no coat-of-arms on the knife handle."

"Then he must have left tracks."

"Storm wiped them. He might have walked on water, for all we know." A backward wave of the hand and he goes on. "Here's what we got: wound to the upper abdomen— nice, clean cut. No other injuries. Toxicology found a nominal amount of alcohol in the bloodstream. Nothing under his fingernails but a few grains of sand."

"Autopsy?"

"His brother made a stink, and anyway the cause of death is clear as a neon sign."

"What about a motive?"

He almost smiles. "Since when has anyone needed a motive to snuff a Yank? They bring it on themselves with their fancy golf clubs, logos, lip—and not just the white ones, anymore. Ugly comes in all colors."

"Stein was no ugly American. Stein was no McCabe. Odd though, the similarities between their deaths."

"Not odd at all. Any Yank serves the purpose, and wasn't Stein Jewish? Those Semitic types are easy to pick out."

Stein's looks, in fact, had been rather Mediterranean. He might have been an Italian film star or a Spanish aristocrat, so chiseled and patrician were his features.

"Odd?" Again, the twinge of a smile. "Someone was having a bad night, that's motive enough."

Above our heads spider monkeys cavort through the

canopy. A green coconut plummets to earth, splits in two, and relinquishes its milk in a puddle at my feet. The informant kicks it aside with the reinforced toe of his combat boot.

"You have my number," I say and veer from him with the anger hot in my eyes.

◆

Biographers there are plenty, most better qualified than I to write the story of Stein's life, but I know this island, know how to chase down facts, who to believe, and I move like a kicked jackass at the least flicker of opportunity (a commodity rare in so small a place).

When, days short of my fortieth birthday—husbandless, without prospects—I left St. Germaine for Miami, I promised myself not to return until I had landed a permanent gig with a news organization several cuts above the *Island Tattler* and earned a master's degree in Philosophy (Stein's suggestion. He thought everyone in the media could benefit from a dollop of Hegel, a double helping of Buber). But life seldom serves up what we wish for, work toward. Instead of a byline with Associated Press, I got stranded in a job licking stamps for the PR director of *Rave International*, a firm dedicated to the proliferation of hip-hop. I enrolled in night school and wieseled my way as far as *I and Thou* before chronic fatigue laid me low. In short, I returned to the island hounded by the same sense of stagnation and failure that had driven me away.

And then Clia called. Francis Stein was dead. It was a tragedy by any measure, but also—call me crass—my long-awaited break, and I was not about to let anyone filch it.

Once I had Stein's notebooks, I had leverage. I could pick up the phone, call any editor, and hold his ear long enough to make my pitch. It seemed expeditious at the time to call Sy Kromsky, Stein's old cohort.

"This is Bat Manley."

"Bat *who*?" The jagged timbre of Kromsky's voice hinted at sleepless nights, chronic heartburn. "What sort of name is that?"

"Look, I'm a friend of Francis Stein. I've just seen him—at the morgue."

Kromsky grew instantly attentive. It had been a while since his last big book and he was hungry. That he was also aggrieved by Stein's murder, I don't mean to understate, but his grief in no way dulled his zest for deal making.

"When can you come to New York?"

It is a coup, yes, but also a cross. The thought of hopping a plane north in deep winter to search for the other half of Stein's life conjures images of black slush, frozen snot. I lie awake nights and grind my molars.

"Stop dis bellyachin'," chides my Aunt Marva, leaning into me with the authority of a woman who knows herself infallible. "For years yah be broker than a bean farmer, now de money fall into your pocket and still de same sad song."

Marva, having assumed by default the maternal yoke left vacant by my mother's premature death from breast cancer, has earned the right to paraphrase and amend my life story. She holds my few sweaters up to the light and fusses with their loose threads. The room grows close with the reek of mothballs.

"But I have no coat."

"Hang dat, the Women's Auxiliary keep a loaner."

Three sizes too large and ten years outmoded.

Marva waits until I retreat to the closet, until my back is turned, then slips a hot water bottle into my half-packed suitcase. An overladen barge of a woman, she is not made for stealth. "I don' know 'bout dis mahn, Stein." Her broad nose creases along the bridge. "All these years on de island and nevah once did he be seen wit' a dark-skin girl."

"After his wife died, he didn't get out much," I reply, but my aunt's remark pricks a nerve and she's quick to note it.

"Didna dat friend of yours, dat Clia, try to mingle yah wit' he?"

"I was married."

"Between your number one an' two. Yah bought dat 'spensive dress and squished your big feet into dem sassy shoes."

It was Clia who had talked me into the shoes, Clia who kept tabs on Stein and pushed me toward him at every fête. He was always polite—flawlessly, to the nth degree. But never once did he ask a personal question, nor did he use the home phone number I found some lame excuse to press on him. "I bought those shoes for Derek's christening."

"Yah wore flats to Derek's christening."

I zip closed my suitcase, shunt it into a corner, and circle my departure date on the Jiffy Brakes wall calendar: January 15, six days hence.

"Not every dead mahn a saint, Batty."

Too tired to mount a defense, I squeeze my aunt's work-worn hand.

"Yah get some sleep." Holding course, she nudges me into my unmade bed and switches out the lamp.

◆

From *Who's Who*, 2000 edition (the last in which Stein appears):

Francis W. Stein 1947—; American author/philosopher. Education: B.A. Sociology, Columbia; M.A. Western Civilization, Columbia; PhD. Ethics, Harvard. Member:

PEN, American Academy of Arts and Letters. Recipient: John D. and Catherine T. MacArthur Award.

Francis Stein, born in Newark, New Jersey, came to prominence during the 1970's when his essays on marginalized groups—anarchists, liberation theologians, street people—began appearing in such publications as the *New York Times*, *Mother Jones*, *The Nation* and others. Stein's essays also aired on Public Broadcast Radio, earning him the weekly spot *Other American Dreams*. His first book, of the same title, appeared in 1973 (Harvard University Press). Stein then crossed genres to write the novel, *Lies that Bind* (Doubleday, 1975), which embroiled him in a libel suit (City of Newark vs Stein); he was later acquitted. There followed in rapid succession *The Despised* (Harper and Row, 1978), *Whose Law, Whose Justice?* (Harper and Row, 1979), *The Myth of Freedom* (Harper and Row, 1980), and *Omissions* (Little, Brown, 1982). He was inducted into the American Academy in 1981 and received the coveted MacArthur "Genius" Award that same year. After the untimely death of his wife Sophie in 1982, Stein endowed a scholarship fund for art students in her name. His collected essays were published by Harvard University Press in 1989.

◆

Sooner than anticipated, I again cross paths with Hugo Fey.

Interesting character, Fey; like Stein a maverick. I met him in the late 80's, when he served as senate minority leader, a post he held vociferously if without effect. His proposals for aid to small-scale cooperatives and socialized healthcare distanced him from the governing elite, who lost no opportunity to undermine his efforts—never in public, for Fey was a master at tongue-lashing his opponents, but via the rumor mill. A murmur of disapproval surrounded him: his blood taint and illegitimacy scandalized the island matriarchs; his foreign education and Marxist leanings posed a threat to his propertied peers. But at our first meeting none of these things concerned me. My paper sent me to interview Fey because he was a bachelor, because he owned a dinner jacket and wore it well. Most of the island's debutantes had been photographed on his arm. Who he would eventually marry remained a topic of speculation for years. And then, long after people had stopped caring, he proposed to my childhood friend Clia Rackham, quietly, only days after Stein's death.

Clia, needing a witness, calls me. Her parents have died, her siblings gone north. She has only her friends and many of these have lately turned from her, irked by her public baiting of Fey. Oddly, Fey himself seems only to find her the more alluring for these assaults. Clia had always been his alter ego, the one person he could not mesmerize with his eloquence. She challenged him as no fawning deb could.

They wed in mourning with black armbands rimming their sleeves. Clia wears a simple dress the color of fennel, Fey an ebony suit. Fey's mother, Jordan, in contrast, decks herself in red satin and the mandatory church hat; she holds the bride's bouquet of orchids in her lace-gloved hands.

"Take them, child," she keeps insisting to Clia. "Tain no sin to be happy on your own weddin' day."

The blooms do little to enliven the proceedings. The justice, roused prematurely from an afternoon doze, reads the ceremony verbatim, the bride and groom say their *I do's*, and Jordan and I sign our names to the marriage certificate. In minutes we are out the door.

"Dis way, dis way..." Jordan leads us through the

narrow, neglected streets of Fabula to her clapboard cottage, built by the mysterious suitor she still refers to as her husband, and throws open the freshly painted gates. Inside mill a dozen or so family members and neighbors, waiting to toast the newlyweds with rationed shots of rum and brimming glassfuls of lemonade. In the background *Moonlight Serenade* drones on an ancient phonograph.

"What took yah so long, Hugo mahn?" chides an elderly relation, leveling his walking cane at the groom as if to flog him. "A beauty like this an' yah keep she on ice?"

Fey glances at his bride then away, through a window, out to sea. "If I could bring back those years…"

Interjects Clia, "It's been a slow thaw."

"An' now yah ripe as a hothouse tomato, yessuh."

Even Fey can't help but smile.

The couple is honeymooning at home. The telephone lies off-hook and the Doberman chained to the front gate sends visitors racing down the road in terror. Respecting their wish for privacy, I tell no one of the wedding and accept with measured patience Fey's repeated evasions.

Only Clia knows the festering wound that is his bereavement. "He doesn't sleep. I find him pacing in the middle of the night with his eyeshade still on. There's something he's keeping from me; I can feel it. He blames himself."

Why? What does he know? If I must lay him open like a skinned possum, I will have my answer.

◆

The Hotel Noir, as much of a home as Stein made for himself on St. Germaine, has not fared well since his death. As the news of the stabbing penetrated its guests' champagne-fogged psyches, they settled their bills and left in a braying exodus. No game show hosts or soccer idols sign autographs in her lobby, no buffed and bejeweled divorcées line her bar. Her marquee glows a dim shade of ginger. Beneath it, a solitary doorman worries the brass buttons on his faded red waistcoat.

I approach the reception desk and ask a dull-eyed attendant for Monsieur Blanc.

"He be ailin'."

"And Madame Blanc?"

He points with his nose toward the far side of the lobby, where the proprietress sits alone sepulchered beneath a hat brim the color of week-old snapper. She speaks into a cell phone propped in the crook of her shoulder and gestures without object. As I draw near, I hear her say, "Our policy clearly states *no pets*, does it not? The hamster must go." She clicks off and sits for a time muttering under her breath.

I step into her shadow and she recoils, lumbers to her feet, and tilts back her boater. Her face, even in silhouette, stuns with its pallor.

"You're keeping well, Madame Blanc."

"You, Bat? Save your flattery. What brings you to the Noir?"

By her tone I know she has not forgiven me for some filler I used a few months ago speculating on her age. This day she might be prehistoric, a stone fetish or pillar of salt. Her blonde tresses hang streaked with gray.

"Francis Stein. I'm writing his biography."

She waves a weary hand. "Well, I suppose you'll do no worse than Blakely or Jones (my colleagues at the *Tattler*)."

"Look, I liked Stein. We all did. This is no dirty secrets book."

She cocks her head and the boater lists as if to capsize. She reseats herself and vaguely motions me into the chair opposite. "I loved him like a brother." Tears seep onto her mascara-caked lashes. "Such a brilliant man, one of the great minds of our era—and to think he sojourned under my roof for all those years! What a privilege. It humbles me to think of it."

"Were you there the night it happened?"

"I retired at midnight to my suite. It was Monsieur Blanc who held Mr. Stein in his arms as he…as he…"

"How long had he been in that state?"

"Hard to say." She rummages in her cleavage for a handkerchief. Her tears have subsided, leaving moony crescents beneath her eyes. "I spoke with him earlier in the evening—how distinguished he looked in his dinner jacket. No one remembers seeing him come back. I personally questioned my entire staff. The horror! The pity. Poor Mr. Stein, even dying he was too polite to call attention to himself."

"May I speak to your husband?"

"He's bedridden. Ulcer, you know. He's been in agony ever since… ever since…"

"Did he say if there were any last words?"

"Mr. Stein's eyes were open, he told me."

"Then he was conscious?"

"Oh yes, to the end. But there was a certain level of hustle and bustle in the room: my husband, hoping to preserve an air of gaiety, had the band turn up their amplifiers. Mr. Stein moved his lips. His voice was very faint. My husband thought he heard—but this is absurd, hardly worth mentioning. My husband thought he heard Mr. Stein say, 'Aren't you going to clap your hands?'"

I laugh, the wrong response.

"You take things too lightly, Bat. But then, you've made a career of poking fun at people. If you ask me, you're out of your league with this." She huffs to her feet. "Let me be crystal clear on one point: I run a respectable establishment. That is all I have to say." Her cell phone vibrates and lowering her chins she vanishes beneath her hat brim.

"Always a pleasure."

I exit through the lounge and comb the poolside. The few guests arrayed there are overweight, overwrought; dribs of catsup and mustard speckle their beach attire. I gaze out toward Shipwreck Cove, the view Stein couldn't get enough of, and imagine him strapping and sunscreened beside his young bride, his Sophie. Their smiles shine brighter than a tropical sun.

◆

From Stein's notebooks:

How to describe an islander's soul? Brackish, yearning vessel only the tides could fill.

◆

My suitcase sits packed and still no word from Hugo. When, at last, Clia returns my calls it is to hold me at bay. "Patience, girlfriend, the honeymoon's just heating up."

"Trying for a new world record? Longest conjugal coitus."

But however much we rib each other, we both know what I'm after and how badly I want it. If anyone understood Francis Stein, if anyone can chart the choreography of his last dance, it is Hugo. Another week goes by before the bridegroom agrees to meet me at Yvette's Sweet Temptations.

He arrives punctually, nods in my direction, and dispensing with small talk drops into the chair opposite me. "Shoot," he says.

"I lost track of Francis back in the early '90s. Even then, he seemed to be withdrawing, turning in on himself. You were the one person he didn't push away."

"Francis didn't want anyone's sympathy." Hugo raises

his coffee cup, puts it down again without drinking. He clears a space on the tabletop and traces circles with a taut fist. "He was not *un*happy these past years. His expectations had contracted. He saw worlds in the little things—a sunset, a good book."

"What about his work? If he wasn't depressed, why didn't he write?"

"Francis had always been at odds with the marketplace. His books were never big sellers. And then the industry started to change, the pressure to write commercially to increase. There was an editor—Crumb something, his name was—who shepherded Francis' early work but gradually grew overbearing. The breaking point was his last book, the one comparing the Jewish and Black Diasporas. For years it consumed Francis, especially after Sophie's death when he needed to escape into something. He took it to Crumb in 90' or 91'—all two thousand pages of it—and the editor told him, great work, now condense it to three hundred and I'll see what I can do."

"So Stein walked?"

"You might say that. He self-published some monographs, used the material in lectures... it reached a certain audience." Hugo stares at the passing trickle of traffic. He has not touched his coffee. "Francis had a whole other life up north, don't forget."

"What do you know about it?"

"Not much. I know he had a brother."

"Marc?"

"Yes, his kid brother. He never mentioned other family, but apparently he had friends, some from his student days, activists, and others from Sophie's circle, artists mostly. He was involved in quite a few causes, the old hell raiser."

"What about women?"

Hugo's eyes flash a warning. "Francis was too much of a gentleman to speak of it."

"I don't doubt that, but years ago didn't he bring some high-class redhead to the Noir? Clia mentioned her once. Peaches-and-cream complexion, Prada handbag, pearls..."

"Back off, Bat. There was no one of any importance after Sophie."

"That Francis Stein loved his wife I'm not debating, but—"

"Next question."

"Your coffee must be cold. Shall I get you another?"

He dismisses the offer with a backhanded wave of his discordantly articulate hands.

"Who killed him, Hugo? What have you told the police?"

"The police? All they want is to get Francis' file off their desks. Even if I had something substantive—which I don't—they would hold to the official line: that Stein got in the way of a domestic dispute. The Chief of Police as much as said that he 'walked into' the knife."

"Had he been drinking?"

"No, he wanted to begin the year sober."

"He wrote to his brother that he'd be home early this season. Why?"

Hugo winces and his scars jog and realign. "I don't know... something was troubling him, *someone*."

"Does the name Veronique mean anything to you?"

"No, should it?"

"There's an odd little poem in his notebook: *Veronique is the sea's flesh, the sun's anchor.* Clia found him buying a necklace. Doesn't sound so much troubled as smitten."

"I'll check the Hall of Records."

"I already did. There's a Veronica Medley in the townships; she'll be eighty-six years old this April."

Hugo sighs and his head sinks low on his gnarled neck. "I thought I knew the man. I thought I knew him."

♦

I shall speak now of Sophie, whose name wasn't Sophie at all but Elizabeth Skye Brenner. Stein alone used the nickname—for what reason, nobody seems to know. In professional circles she went by Skye, among family by Liz. A languid, malleable woman, she adopted a mien appropriate to each.

Stein and his Sophie… he carried himself taller in her presence, gestured more lavishly, laughed more readily. She was helium to his gravity, not so much frivolous as good-natured. A pleaser.

Stein missed no opportunity to nudge her into the spotlight. "Meet the inimitable Mrs. Stein. Perhaps you've seen her work: she's been compared to Picasso, but I say she outshines the old man by a million watts."

She would widen her blue eyes, toss her golden curls. "My one fan."

Comparisons to the greats notwithstanding, Stein's wife never amounted to more than a minor talent. Her posthumous fame, my sources agree, had more to do with her association with Stein and his relentless efforts at promotion than with the deftness or originality of her canvasses. The artist she might have become, we will never know. Her very brushstrokes suggest inquiry. She died at the age of twenty-five.

To please Stein I interviewed her once for the women's page. She stood waist high in water at the shallow end of the swimming pool, wearing a vivid cerulean swimsuit that accentuated her youth.

"What brings you and your husband back to St.

Germaine?" I began by asking.

"The light." She dipped down at the knees until her chin floated just above the water line. "For me, it's the light. Francis enjoys the people, the music—he's won the hotel's limbo contest three years running."

"Do you paint while you're here?"

"I sketch."

"Does your husband write?"

"He daydreams."

"May we expect you next season?"

"Absolutely." She rose, glistening, to her full height. "Francis and I are talking about finding a place of our own here."

I lowered my note pad. "There's a bungalow for sale near me, nothing fancy. You might want to fix it up."

"Francis, did you hear? Bat knows a place."

Later that day I took them there. Sophie had changed into a loose-fitting sundress with spaghetti straps; Stein sported a Panama. The drive took us north past the outdoor market, the rum factory, and one of St. Germaine's poorer districts, known to the locals as Yam Flats.

Stein grew quiet.

I gestured out the window. "What the cruise ship crowd *doesn't* see."

"You would think with all the revenue generated by tourism something more could be done for these people."

The remark struck me as naïve, but I said nothing. Sophie, alert to the slightest shift of mood, swiveled in her seat. "This piece of coast has a wildness about it—can't you feel it? And not a single golf course. Look at those breakers!"

It would have been hard to brood in her presence. She was good for Stein, the spark that kept him from floundering in his own darkness. He turned his gaze where she directed and the smile soon returned to his face.

We arrived at the bungalow with the sun overhead and a gentle breeze rippling the tall grasses. Sophie slipped on sunglasses and bolted from the car, crying, "Have you ever seen such views!" Stein caught up with her and the two embraced, kissed, as if oblivious of my presence.

I stood at the door, poised to open it and show them around. They, holding hands, lingered on the grounds.

"We'll build you a studio here, a sundeck there—and the nursery, Mrs. Stein? Where would you like the nursery?"

Sophie blushed and one hand came to rest on her softly rounded belly. She glanced in my direction, replete in a way the confirmed barren will never know. In that moment she carried the future and all its giddy possibility within her.

◆

From Stein's notebooks:

Lovers rode the waves, children splashed in the surf, and a jellyfish, solitary, floated in the shallows, gazing up at the sky and seeing endless peril—how do birds not drown in such a sky?

◆

To walk the streets of New York feels like treading the body of an island-sized trauma victim. My nerves cannot field all the mutant impulses projected onto me by chrome and glass. Every manhole, every subway station, every revolving door opens to me like a jaw. Kromsky's office lies at the center of things, midtown, with a view toward the void recently vacated by the World Trade Center. There is nothing grand about the place; in fact, the rooms are cramped, dingy, and smell of decades-old takeout—as does Kromsky himself.

"Coffee?" he says by way of greeting.

His secretary, giving me a studied once-over, deposits a Styrofoam cup into my hand. Its heat helps thaw the fingers.

"Well, what have you got for me?"

"A quandary."

"Sounds like something Francis would have said."

"I'm flattered."

"Don't be." Kromsky muffles a sigh with his chapped knuckles. "Francis made life hard for himself. For years I begged the guy, give me something commercial, give me something I can sell. But no, to him *commercial* was a dirty word. How to generate buzz about a book the length of an encyclopedia comparing Blacks to Jews? Does John Q. Public give a flying fu'—excuse my French—about displaced minorities?"

"Maybe not, but Stein obviously did."

"Yes, he did. He cared. He cared to a fault, but publishing is not a forgiving business. Okay, so he won a couple highbrow awards, but did that spare him from the remainders table? Did it earn him the readership he deserved?" Kromsky fences with his ballpoint. "The guy had everything—brains, moral stature, a razor-sharp point of view—he towered over all these lightweights on the bestseller list, and what did he do with all that talent? Pissed it away on some sleepy little island."

I quash the urge to defend my natal home; too much at stake. "If you mean that Stein produced little finished work on St. Germaine, yes, it appears that he wrote only snippets. A manuscript may yet surface."

"His brother has already been through his papers: more snippets."

"Look, I didn't want to tell you this on the phone, but—Stein's notebooks, there's something quite uncanny about them. He seems to have been compiling a book about St. Germaine, and yet *not*. It seems that he saw the island as a stage upon which a much larger drama was unfolding: the new world order in microcosm, an equatorial *War and Peace...*"

"Bit grandiose, wouldn't you say?"

I tone down. "The entries alternate between actual and fictional events. He followed the local news more closely than one might expect of so cosmopolitan a man, ferreted out the universals."

"What's so extraordinary about that? Stein had been doing it for years."

"But the entries—sometimes they recount events, and sometimes they foretell them."

Kromsky lumbers to his feet, begins to pace. "What are you getting at?"

"I'm not sure..." *Lame, Bat. You're losing him.*

"There's got to be a logical explanation for it," the editor ruminates. "Stein was absentminded, never good on dates."

"The dates correlate with his dream journal. The dreams themselves, some of them, are prophetic."

"Dreams?"

"Nightmares may be more accurate—he recorded them—a dozen or more, spanning the last two months of his life."

The editor jars to a halt. "Look, you're heading down a blind alley with all this. Francis was an intellectual, not some navel gazer. Francis lived in the real world. To portray him as a tormented prophet would be a disservice. And besides, we're not a New Age press."

"But—" *Stein can't be neatly classified, stuck on a shelf. The man he became was not the man you knew.*

"Just stick to the facts."

"Right." *The facts according to Bat Manley.*

Kromsky drops back into his desk chair and swivels

wearily toward me. "We can't afford to waffle. After Sophie's death Francis let himself get sidetracked and his name passed into obscurity like yesterday's fad diet. Some psycho stabs a kitchen knife into his gut, and suddenly he's James Dean. You were a newspaper hack, weren't you? Think like one now. Give me a story."

◆

Postcard, dated December 28

Dear Marc,

Change of plan: will be returning to MA shortly after the 1ˢᵗ of the year. Please keep it quiet for now, as there's some research I hope to do before resuming the social whirl.

Look forward to catching up.

All the best,
Francis

◆

I call Marc Stein from a phone booth in Times Square to let him know I'll be taking a commuter flight to Boston the following day. He has one of those voices that melt on the lobe, soft, mellifluous, with a perpetual lilt of curiosity.

"Bat? Short for Batia, the Pharaoh's daughter who rescued Moses from the Euphrates?"

"I'm afraid not."

"For Bathsheeba, King David's concubine and mother to a scion of Israel?"

"No, just Bat."

"I don't recall Francis having mentioned you." A less tactful man would accuse me of stretching the truth. "Well, I suppose you have the address…"

We arrange to meet at his home, a row house on the South End, one of the few that hasn't been renovated. Pigeon droppings fleck its tatty facade. There is an air of history about the place, of cabals and public hangings. A cemetery graces the nearby churchyard, its slate and granite headstones strafed with graffiti.

Marc is more reserved in person, not unfriendly but mindful of the power of words—like his older brother Francis. I have the impression that he measures me; his red-rimmed eyes leave mine only to glance out a bay window edged in frost. "How Francis hated the northern winters, even as a boy." He helps me off with my borrowed coat. His nearness smells faintly of wood smoke and printer's ink.

"You must still be in shock. How did the news reach you?"

"A young woman called. She didn't give her name. She said she was a friend of Francis then she broke down and wept."

"Is that all?"

"I asked, is he ill? And she said, *mortally* ill—odd use of language for a young person, wouldn't you say? She hung up before I could get details. A couple of hours later the official call came from the coroner and soon after another from Hugo Fey. Perhaps you know Hugo. From what Francis told me, he's a man of unusual courage."

"That he is," I concede.

"Then you do know him?"

"Fey's not an easy man to know. Some people hide behind their reputations, others behind their scars."

A moment's silence while his eyes drift again to the uncurtained window. "I never made it to St. Germaine. Francis invited me a hundred times, but I always had other commitments."

"That anonymous caller... had Francis ever mentioned a woman?"

We are still standing in the foyer, Marc holding the Auxiliary's horse-blanket overcoat and I massaging the circulation back into my hands.

"Come, I'll make a fire."

I follow him across an Indian kilim patterned in muted reds and golds and up a narrow staircase lined with bookshelves, scanning titles as I ascend: *Pilgrim of the Absolute, Parallel Proverbs, Job's Dungheap, Echoes of the Hasidic Soul...* "You have quite a collection of Theology."

"Tools of the trade. I'm a rabbi, you know."

My feet miss a step.

"You knew Francis was Jewish, didn't you?" He waves me across a threshold into a comfortable, if sparsely furnished, den.

"I assumed he was. His religion didn't seem particularly relevant. I thought of him, first and foremost, as a humanist."

Marc sighs audibly. With back turned he stacks logs onto the fireplace grate. His heartbreak voice drifts back, "Francis' disaffection for organized religion in no way cut him off from the rich vein of philosophy and social discourse that runs through Jewish culture. His humanism was an outgrowth of his ethical formation as a Jew."

"Without God?"

Marc turns to face me, his upturned palms dimpled where knots of wood have grazed them. "My brother was not an atheist. He had doubts... don't we all? It was hard for him to grasp how a world so fraught with pain could be the creation of an all-knowing Lord. The patriarchal model chafed him. He had great respect for the feminine qualities so undervalued in Western society. Our mother saw to that."

The tinge of a smile softens the set of his generous lips. "Please, sit down. I'll bring you a cup of tea."

Left alone, I take a spiral notebook from my handbag and jot, *Marc Stein: brother's spiritual counterpart (foil?), not at all what I'd expect of a rabbi. Same elegant good looks as Francis but without the tan. His guard is up—why?*

"I hope you like peppermint?" He clears unopened mail from an end table and sets down a lacquered tray.

I thank him and replace the notebook in my purse. "You haven't answered my question, if there was a woman."

"The omission was intentional. Look, Bat, I'm not entirely comfortable with this. My brother was a private person. Had he wanted to make intimate disclosures about himself, he would have published a memoir."

I had expected resistance. "Francis Stein embraced a public life as well, he had a readership. Your brother's biography *will* be written. Wouldn't you rather it be written by someone who knew and admired him?"

He cradles his head in his hands, large expressive hands like Francis'. "I'm just trying to do the right thing."

We sit for a moment in silence. The fire begs tending, but my host doesn't seem to notice.

"Okay, tell me about yourself," he says abruptly.

"What would you like to know?"

"Start from the beginning—family, education. You must have attended church?"

"I was born in '59, a good year for cane. My father was an overseer for United Fruit. The bottom fell out of the sugar industry when I was still a girl and we became poor like everybody else. Luckily, I had brothers. The two oldest went to work on a freighter and sent money home. My mother insisted I stay in school. She wasn't about to see me end up a chambermaid. She'd had little schooling herself—there was no university on the island until her turn had passed. But I must be boring you."

"Not at all."

"My mother's favorite adage was, 'The Lord helps those who help themselves.' We prayed with our shirtsleeves rolled up. Sure we went to church, everyone did back then: Prince Chapel Methodist Gospel Church, where Jesus is Lord and anyone caught smoking on the Sabbath can expect to be shamed into abstinence. I had two church dresses, one for normal Sundays and another for Easter, Christmas and when I had to walk the collection basket up to the altar."

"Have you remained a believer?"

"Assuming I ever was one. Children don't believe or disbelieve. Their world is magical not spiritual, and surely not religious."

He nods faintly then knits his fingers. "Still, one has a foundation, a framework upon which to build."

"In the best case."

"Have you children of your own?"

"No—no, I wasn't blessed that way. My first husband couldn't have them, and my second… well, he wouldn't have made much of a father."

Marc reaches over and pats my hand, an awkward gesture. "I'm sorry," he murmurs.

I wait for him to quote scripture, to say something cryptic or saccharine or impossibly wise, but he only sits watching me.

"Any more questions, rabbi?"

His shoulders curl forward. "Who killed my brother?"

"If I knew…"

"I would like to believe this was not about race. Francis Stein, a one-man crusade for human rights, murdered for being white?"

"Hatred doesn't spare the innocent."

"Is that what you intend to say in your book?"

"I'm a reporter, not a preacher. I lay out the facts and let people draw their own conclusions."

"Facts are paltry things. My brother was more than the sum of his credentials and frequent flyer miles: he had a noble soul. Can you capture that on paper?"

"I can sure as hell try."

Marc sits back in his chair, stroking his beardless chin. "You sound like Francis."

I smile despite myself. "You're not the first person to tell me that."

The rasp of a door opening, of soft-soled shoes shuffled on a doormat. Marc glances at his wristwatch. "My partner is home early. Excuse me a moment." He walks hurriedly out into the hallway, closing the door behind him.

The wood fire flickers, the room dims. I take the notebook from my purse and quickly scribble, *Getting no-where. Rabbi testing me. I'm doing most of the talking.*

Marc returns within moments but does not take a seat. "Something's come up," he says in a tone part apology, part dismissal. "How long will you be in town?"

"Until tomorrow," I say, though I have no fixed itinerary.

"Try me late morning. You have my number."

The urge to clutch at his sleeve propels me across the room before I can collect myself. "I need you, Marc. I need you to help me solve the puzzle—your brother's life on the island, up here... the pieces don't fit together."

"I can't hand you the cipher of Francis' existence. I'm sorry, but I really have to go now." He opens the door and steps aside to let me pass. His footsteps echo after me like the plaint of a choir drum.

◆

Postcard, dated December 28:

Greetings, Bill,

Still want that rematch? My chess game is as rusty as an old corkscrew; here's your chance for an easy win.

Would you mind turning on the heat in the townhouse? I should be back the first week of January, just in time to wish you a bon voyage as you sail for Bermuda.

Best Regards,
Francis

◆

"We did things like that for each other—fiddle with the climate control, start the car, water the plants. Francis didn't have any actually, plants, but I do. Have you seen his place? Talk about Spartan: wall-to-wall books, a laptop and a bed."

"Do you mind if I take notes?"

"Not at all."

William O'Bride: neighbor, financial advisor, schoolmate from Harvard days... appears not to have made it to Bermuda. Peaked. Looks older than Francis.

"I'd like to see Francis' townhouse while I'm here."

"I have a key, but I'd need to ask Marc. The place is his now." He lights up a Rothman's, blows the smoke over his shoulder. "How Francis used to get on my case."

"About?"

He motions toward a dirty ashtray. "Who'd have thought I would outlive him?"

Outside it is snowing. In O' Bride's office the central

heating induces the illusion of perpetual summer: potted sago palms slouch above the sand-colored Berber, a humidifier softly gurgles.

"Marc held a memorial service last week—I suppose he told you? Guys I hadn't seen in thirty years flew in from Aspen, from Big Sur... not many of us stayed in the Boston area after grad school. Now there's the estate to settle." He pauses to exhale. "So, what do you want to know?"

"The Stein of the 60's, what was he like?"

O'Bride swivels in his desk chair, stands up, and begins to pace in expanding ellipses. "Francis didn't exactly put his body upon the wheels—we had the SDS for that—but he spoke out against the war and the general bullshit of that era every chance he got. Let's say he *flirted* with radical politics. Ten thousand of us went out on strike, the hubris of it, and the whole time Francis kept saying, 'You want to know who mints our diplomas? The Pentagon, that's who.' Then he backhanded the administration with his thesis: *Higher Education and Military Research.* It was Harvard scientists who created napalm, don't forget."

"You kept in touch after graduation?"

"On and off. Francis was something of a hermit when he was writing, and then winters he'd disappear altogether. We grew closer once I got into finance; he was one of my first clients."

"Weren't you a Philosophy major?"

"That's right."

"Quite a switch."

He faces me, a look of umbrage straining his smile. "Not at all. Socially responsible investing is my line. I help people put their money where their ideals are. Francis, for example, did not want to support any company that produced arms or that dumped toxic waste or... the list goes on and on."

Had O'Bride pegged wrong. How to get back on his good side?

"Francis had scruples all right. Unloaded AT&T the moment he heard they overcharged inmates."

"I see what you were up against."

"Dropped Citigroup—gas development in the Peruvian Amazon."

"Stein too perfect. What was his fatal flaw?"

"The hardest part wasn't figuring out where to put his money but curbing his manic generosity. I suppose you heard about the foundation he started when Sophie died? Chunk of bread, that."

"And his estate?"

"Not worth much. Marc gets the house, the car, some spare change for his flock; the rest gets divvied-up among Francis' pet causes."

O'Bride drops back into his desk chair, and with the filter of his smoked-down cigarette still clamped between his lips reaches for another. "Now I have a question for you. How does a man go through twenty-five thousand dollars in a single month on St. Germaine? I know things can be pricey in-season, but still."

$25,000 bucks. Fishy... "The Noir upgraded its wine list, I've heard."

He takes aim with a cocked index finger. "That's a lot of wine, my friend. You don't buy that explanation any more than I do."

"No way," I have to admit. "I'll look into it, Mr. O'Bride."

"Bill."

"I'll look into it—Bill."

"That's better. Formality can be so... formal." His

nicotine-stained fingers inch across the desk to explore the contours of my wrist. His gaze hovers at the level of my bosom. "What hotel are you staying at? Let me give you a lift."

"Thanks, but I have another appointment."

"Dinner then."

I stand and pull on my oversized coat, the better to shelter my assets.

Snuffing out his Rothman's, he exhales hard. "Never did have Francis' sex appeal. Try not to hold it against me, eh?"

◆

Marc isn't at home when I call the next morning. His answering machine wishes me *shalom* and cuts off amid a crescendo of beeps.

"Please, I really must speak to you. I'm staying at the Parker House—darn, can't find the number. Marc? *Anyone?*"

A frigid wind whips through the city, sweeping the clouds inland, leaving the sidewalks one continuous sheet of ice. Slush lines the curbs. The weather channel has forecast snow, several feet of it, and people trudge through the street with their heads lowered and hats flying off like crows.

I stop in Filene's Basement and buy a pair of gloves, the type that start out small and grow to the size of your fingers. A man with stubble on his chin and cheap whiskey on his breath shadows me up and down the aisles whispering, "Spare a smoke? A buck? Sell you a tip on a horse?"

At the exit I turn to glare at him.

"Peace," he says, shrinking from me in mock terror.

I feel the cold migrate inside of me. On the street once again I race skidding to a crowded intersection and hurl myself upon a taxi. The cabby's hand reaches on reflex for the meter flag before asking, "Where to?"

A professor to whom Stein dedicated his first book, Jacob Lesch, is the only other person I absolutely need to see in Boston. Settling myself in the passenger seat, I give the cabbie a Roxbury address.

The taxi stops in front of a drab building on a lightless side street.

"This is it," says the driver, pointing.

"A facility for the criminally insane? There must be some mistake."

He repeats the address aloud, points again, this time with blatant irritation. I crumple a bill into his fingerless mitten and step out into an arctic chill. As the taxi speeds away I check the address against the one scribbled in my notebook—a match, unmistakably—and make my way up a concrete ramp.

"Help you?" chirps a blonde woman in uniform, reluctantly buzzing me in.

A fetid smell drives me back a step. An acne-faced rookie with a conspicuous holster urges, "Come on, come on, you're letting in the cold."

"Mr. Lesch?"

"I'll check the visitor list," says the blond, already bending over a sheath of stamped papers. "You Ms. Manley? Been here before?"

"First time."

"Lucky for you Lesch was just reclassified low security. Wait there." She steps out of her glass cubicle and runs a hand-held security device along my clothes front, back and sides. The rookie inspects the contents of my purse.

"What's Lesch in for?"

"He'll tell you. Old commie loves to mouth-off."

She leads me down an airless corridor to a visiting room, where Lesch—white-haired, jowly—sits at a metal table chatting with his orderly. "Step into my office," he says with inflated irony, motioning me toward a chair. "Place stinks, huh? I get out so rarely I hardly notice it anymore."

"Beats the street on a day like this."

"Yeah, a veritable monument to the human spirit." He squares his elbows on the table edge and for a moment a grimace of pain replaces the jokester smile. "Now, let's talk about Francis."

Before I can frame a first question he launches into a monologue. "Francis was a human being. When he was in town he'd come by to visit every week and we'd play chess—he'd let me win. Never had much fight in him. I wouldn't say he was my most brilliant student, but he had a social conscience, something lacking in the rest. He made a mission of giving voice to the people society brands as undesirables and casts aside. He understood them—why? Because, although he moved with apparent ease in some very select circles, he was never of them. He was not an academic, not some pop guru, not a Mailer or a Roth—he hadn't their swagger, their puerile need for the spotlight. He was actually a rather shy person. I think he would have been happiest living on that island with Sophie, writing a book now and then, having children…"

"What was it you taught?"

"The course was called *The Individual in Society*, but what I taught was integrity. Then, as now, a million forces competed for our souls. In those days anyone who raised a picket sign was called a radical. Yet under that umbrella co-existed a multiplicity of ideologies—pacifists, utopians, Maoists, etc… and a whole lot of people, who without icons or grandiose schemes, questioned the status quo and were willing to take a stab at something better. Francis and I fell into that latter category, if any." He scratches his hairless pate. "What were we talking about?"

"Integrity."

"Right. Francis was hard on himself. I don't think he saw himself as an especially good person—he held himself to high standards, impossible standards. In fact, he berated himself for not doing enough. With so much need in the world, so much injustice, even a compassionate person must draw the line, say 'I can do so much and no more.' For Francis that line was never clear, and he suffered for it."

An attendant in a cotton lab coat and baggy trousers approaches with a tray. "Your cocktail, hon'," she says brightly and hands Lesch a Dixie cup filled with a chalky pink liquid.

He colors slightly. "Leave it there, Margie, if you would. I'm in conference." He gestures with his chin toward the table and forces a smile. "As I was saying…"

"Francis suffered."

"Yes, he felt keenly the way the world was going, the mindless consumerism, the growing intolerance… it immobilized him, the harshness of things. *No fight.* And he wasn't alone: Every era has its casualties, the would-be saints who give too much. One day they wake up and there's nothing left of them but a shell." Lesch taps a slippered foot against the table leg. "There are worse things than dying young."

"I must be tiring you."

"A beautiful young woman tiresome? Never." He laughs suddenly. "Here's Francis for you: At my sentencing—twenty-five to life, go figure—he jumps to his feet and starts shouting, "Where's the justice? What are we, a pack of Huns?" *Huns…*" Again Lesch laughs and doubles over, as if to expel glass shards from his throat. "Only Francis would have come out with a thing like that."

"Mr. Lesch, if you don't my asking—"

"What's a smart guy like me doing in a place like this, right? Rush Limbaugh. I wanted to kill the shmuck. My mistake was to talk about it. The FBI doesn't distinguish among modes of discourse. It's all literal to them."

"But you don't seem crazy."

"Crazy beats dead, dig? How long would an old pussy like me last in a high-security prison?" Lesch glances toward the orderly, who stifles a yawn. "So, you're from St. Germaine? Francis was writing something down there, I think. He wouldn't say much about it. He couldn't quite get a handle on it, whatever it was…"

◆

From Stein's notebooks:

The island hospital sits empty. The local balmist has a cure for everything—rheumatism, melancholy, the shakes… all in Mason jars, all in a row. But I can't name my malady; it has been with me too long, curled up in a corner like an old hound. Only at night does it show its yellow teeth

◆

Eager to fill my lungs with air that smells of something other than urine or baked beans, I walk the shoveled streets, the icy urban parks. My limbs grow numb, not an unpleasant sensation at first. I drop onto a bench and rub them briskly with my gloved hands. As I gaze about deciding where best to hail a taxi, a familiar landmark comes into view: a church cemetery, its leaning headstones vandalized. My feet skate toward it. Row houses to either side of me, one façade indistinguishable from the next. After several near-tumbles I collide with a wrought iron banister, at the end of which Marc's front door peeks out from a valance of icicles.

There is no public telephone in view, so I knock at the door, gingerly at first, like the uninvited visitor I am. No

142

response. I pace a few stiff steps and double back. The sky has turned the color of iron and a blue-edged snow has begun to fall.

I lean against the banister, every pore burning with cold. I shrink low into my coat collar, stamp my feet, picture the hearth in Marc's den—surely he will be home soon, heaping logs onto the grate.

The wind takes on fury, obliterates in a moment what remains of daylight. I gaze down the narrow residential street but can see no farther than the next doorstep.

"Excuse me?" A male voice, soft like Marc's but higher-pitched. "If you're waiting for Marc... I suppose you'd better come in." He unlocks the door, steps aside to allow me through. "I could call you a taxi."

"When do you expect Marc?"

"With this blizzard there's no telling." He walks about the foyer, shedding his bomber jacket and scarf, switching on an unmatched assortment of lamps. "But your shoes are caked with ice. Here, slip into these." He takes a pair of sheepskin slippers from the closet.

"Don't trouble yourself."

"Nonsense. Put these on—you're not from up north, are you?"

"I'm from St. Germaine."

"Wasn't that where...?"

"I knew Francis."

"Follow me."

I pad behind him up the well-read stairs: *God in Freedom, Lamentations Rabbah, Guide for the Perplexed...*

"Den's the warmest room in the house."

"Do you live here?"

He gazes over a shoulder. At close range his eyes hold a glint of irony. "Where else would I live? I'm Marc's partner."

I stub a toe.

"Careful. These old staircases are awfully steep." He settles me in the same armchair I had occupied during my visit with Marc and sets to work on the fire. "You're Bat, aren't you? I'm Reyn. Look, before you start asking a lot of questions, you might as well know: Marc isn't at all cool with this. Ever since you first called he's been going on about the 'unwanted gaze'—it's from the Talmud: 'Even the smallest intrusion into private space by the unwanted gaze causes damage, because the injury caused cannot be measured.'"

"The media abides by secular law."

"Marc has gone there too. He could quote Brandeis in his sleep: 'The common law secures to each individual the right of determining to what extent his thoughts, sentiments and emotions shall be communicated to others.'"

"Wasn't it Brandeis who called the function of the press *almost holy*?" The idea, handily culled from Journalism 101, elicits nothing more from Reyn than a shrug. He strikes a match against the mantel.

"No doubt Marc would have a comeback; I'm clean out. We have always kept a bit of a distance where his brother's public life is concerned, not wanting to..."

"I understand."

"Do you?" The kindling flashes, revealing a deeper fire smoldering in the gray-green facets of Reyn's eyes. He goes on, "Not wanting to be seen as the stigmatized and shunted-aside victims his brother used to write about."

"I don't recall Francis having published anything on gay rights."

"He didn't. Francis collected causes, but Marc let him know that we were perfectly capable of agitating for our own rights. Marc's one concession was to let his brother march beside us every year in the Pride parade." Reyn takes a seat opposite me and glances at his wristwatch. "Traffic must be grisly with this snow."

"I suppose their differing spiritual views imposed a certain distance?"

"Look, I've already said too much." He gets to his feet with a gangly grace. "I'd better get working on dinner. Help yourself to a book." He gestures toward the shelves that line three sides of the room from floor to ceiling: *Children of the Ghetto, Midrash, Book of Delight...*

I must doze. The fire has burned to embers and Marc is kneeling before it. He seems to sense my gaze on his back, for he says in a low voice, "Rest. Dinner will be ready soon."

"I don't mean to impose."

"We're snowbound, a rare evening at home." He is quiet, almost somber, and continues to stare into the flames even once his stoking has brought the fire back to life. "I hope you like vegan fare. Reyn works for an animal welfare organization."

"You didn't return my calls."

He crosses the room without haste, drag-legged, his chin grazing the nap of his rag wool sweater. He does not seat himself. "A man died, someone I had been preparing for ordination. He knew he had AIDS—we all knew—but the disease progressed so quickly. He wanted to die a rabbi."

"I'm sorry."

"The ground is too frozen to bury him."

We observe silence until Reyn appears in the doorway. "Dinner's ready. I hope Bat likes tofu."

"She's forewarned," Marc says, a smile lighting on his lips and leaving them just as quickly. "It's a good night to try that Haute Brion Francis left with us."

We file down the staircase. Reyn has put a CD in the player, something lovesick with conspicuous bass; candles adorn the dining room table; baking smells waft from the kitchen.

"You'll have to excuse me… my gloom tonight, and—my brother would have been fifty-five next week. How would he have celebrated, I wonder?"

What had he left to celebrate?

Marc excuses himself and detours to the kitchen sink. Bobbing over his soaped hands, he appears to talk to himself.

"Ritual," Reyn explains. "He's praying."

Before we dine the rabbi blesses the bread and the wine, recites a prayer over them in a throaty language I take to be Hebrew, then, intelligible again, he prompts me, "Eat, enjoy."

Reyn serves. "So, you were a friend of Francis?"

"We socialized. Of course, Francis kept to himself more and more as the years went on. We all did. There was a time when the people of my island were eager to mix with visitors, isolated out in the sea as we are. That's changed. Today, with cruise ships and all-inclusive resorts, the tourists need never cross paths with a native, apart from the maid or bellman—de facto, apartheid."

Marc nods. "Francis spoke of it."

"Your brother was no herd animal. He didn't care that St. Germaine had ceased to be fashionable twenty years ago. He took the time to know us. He had an islander's soul."

An islander's soul," Marc echoes. "Yes, I believe you're right."

"Wine?" asks Reyn.

The glasses fill, the music drones; in such an ambience, it would be easy to forget the dead, to dwell in the senses without past or future. But Francis is present. I see him in Marc's fraught shoulders, hear him in the blue notes.

"I've been wondering about the name of your island."

"Jesuit missionaries. When Jesus Christ didn't float our boat, they brought out the whole panoply of saints. Germaine's the one that finally made converts of us."

"Curious phenomenon."

"Not really. We're pariahs, just as she was: not black enough, not white, colonized and forsaken a dozen times."

Mark pauses his fork. "But why a European saint? Surely there were deities for export in Africa?"

"Was Moses gay?"

"I get your point."

"Of course, Germaine can't work her miracles without the trickster Anansi. Anansi is darkness to her light, and shrewd. There's no getting the better of him."

"Like a politician," says Reyn, grinning as he refills my glass.

Pleads Marc, "Let's not start on politics."

"Remember how Francis used to speculate that Laura Bush was actually a life-sized wax doll?"

The atmosphere might be one all-engulfing sigh.

"I'll put on java," Reyn says and disappears into the kitchen."

"How do you like the Haute Brion?" asks Marc, staring at the label with a look of—what? Disdain, or is it simple sadness? Our eyes meet, folded by optics into deceptive union, on the curvature of the bottle's svelte neck. "Francis has left me quite a cellar, not that I know one vintage from another. The gift is wasted on me."

Mark turns away. For the first time since hunting him down I ask myself by what entitlement I am here, intruding on his mourning, probing its raw heart.

He sets down his glass, pushes it aside. "The townhouse I'll sell—Reyn's organization could use an infusion of cash—but the wine?"

"Perhaps I should call a cab."

"No, it's time we talk. After coffee."

◆

We are back in the den, Marc and I. It must be ten, maybe later; I should be tired but I'm not. The fire blazes. My joints thaw and I meld with the seat cushions, savoring the sofa's worn plush. Marc lingers crouched at the hearth before perching at the edge of his accustomed seat.

"I've decided to take a chance on you, Bat."

I must quash the urge to lunge for my steno-pad.

"Take notes, tape the conversation… accuracy is important. All I ask is that you try not to embellish. Francis would have hated that."

I fish the recorder from my handbag and in my eagerness fumble with all the wrong buttons. "Be right with you."

He waits in silence.

"Where to begin? Perhaps if you'd just speak to me about your childhood, about growing up with Francis."

His torso slumps forward, carrying his gaze to a puddled shadow on the floor. "Francis was older by four years, big for his age, and good at everything—school, sports. Funny thing, though, he always seemed to come in second. If he ran for class president, he'd finish second; same with tennis tournaments, essay contests… He'd make jokes about it, like the Avis commercial. I wouldn't say he lacked motivation, but he was no alpha male."

"No doubt he had his own measure of success?"

"I hadn't thought about it. Perhaps, it had something to do with how much a person is willing to risk to do good."

"Is that Francis' view or you own?"

"I'd say we arrived at the same conclusion. Francis was political, as you know, for many years; even recently, when nudged into action. People were always asking him to serve on this and that task force or campaign. He rarely said no, but he emerged from each battle more disillusioned with the machinery of government. In his last essays he spoke increasingly of the personal bond and the wisdom of bypassing large entities. Critics accused him of 'late onset provincialism.' It wasn't that at all. Francis was saying, look around you, honor the impulse to do good. Society can't legislate conscience."

"Tell me something about your parents."

"They were first-generation Americans, both of them, zealous Democrats. My father worked a couple of jobs until he'd saved enough to open a shoe store—Francis was always very particular about his shoes. Even as a student he shined his loafers." Marc pauses and his eyes glaze over. "My mother kept the books, not a penny got by her. We lived in Newark until…" A one-shouldered shrug. "We stayed on longer than most white families."

"And then?"

"The burbs. Francis was fifteen when we moved, old enough to bemoan the loss of his Black and Hispanic friends, the loss of streets and storefronts and the window they gave him on lives so different from our own. The local library offered a puny collection, but at that age he wasn't picky about his reading. He read cereal boxes. He had no one with whom to discuss Hesse or Nabokov, no standard against which to judge what he read. Later, he would write that he came of age in an 'intellectual bingo parlor.' College was his ticket out. At seventeen he was accepted to Columbia and spent the next six years in Manhattan—that's where he met Sophie, at her first gallery showing."

"And you, Marc? Where were you during those years?"

He jars upright. "Look, I thought this was my brother's

book."

"What I meant was, did you see much of Francis? Were you close?"

"I pulled away—from family, from my own brother—for a while. It was later, once Francis had relocated to New England, that we came back together. My father had sold the store by then. I had struck out on my own. Having missed the crest of the Sixties, there was no clear path for me. I was seeking, doing the Eastern thing, and had yet to find my calling. Francis urged me to come to Boston. He took me in and hired me as a researcher, part-time, while I 'found myself'—that was the phrase he used."

"And Sophie?"

"Sophie called me her guru. Having grown up the only child of atheist parents, spirituality was terribly exotic to her." The memory leaves a wistful smile on his face.

"Francis must have had feelings of his own about your search?"

"He never discouraged me, not then and not later when I decided to enter seminary, but those realms don't speak to everyone. For many years it was a source of sorrow to me, that my brother, the best person I have known, should live shut off from the divine current—not shut off in his thinking, but in some more fundamental way. Comfortless."

"Surely you tried to enlighten him?"

"We Jews have never been evangelists, and Francis and I respected each other too much to resort to persuasion. Besides—"

The tape runs out with a loud click.

Marc glances at his wristwatch. "I'll prepare the guest room."

"Not yet. Please. You were saying?"

"Francis put me through seminary, hadn't I mentioned

that? He'd just won an award—the MacArthur, I think it was. By the time I graduated Sophie was gone and my brother had had enough of this house. He saw her in every room, in every object… it was tearing him apart. So, again, I found myself the beneficiary of his preternatural generosity." He motions about him vaguely indicating the walls, and then draws his arms tight against his sides. "I had only one thing to give in return: a connection to some higher power—call it what you will—the sole faculty nature had denied him. If only he had let me."

The hearth's last embers burn to ash. For what seems a long time we sit swaddled in darkness, in the dwindling warmth, each chained to a separate hurt.

"There's something you're bound to find out," Marc says at last, "something… delicate, and I'd rather you hear it from me. Leave the recorder off. Just listen." Marc gets to his feet and takes a few aimless paces. "The best people go through difficult patches. The best people *crack*. Francis wasn't himself after Sophie's death. He'd wanted so much to be a father." The rabbi reaches up and swipes away a tear. "Francis withdrew. Months would go by without a call. Finally, I arrived home one day to a message: my brother, telling me he was okay, not to worry, but he had checked himself into a rehab center for a couple of weeks. Rehab? He'd never in his life drunk alcohol or touched drugs."

"What was he treated for?"

"I never knew the details. The doctor had prescribed something after Sophie's death—a sedative? An anti-depressant? Whatever it was, either Francis took too much or mixed it with wine or…? Anyway, he was cured in three weeks and never relapsed. *Never*. You have my word."

"And you expect me to sweep the episode under the carpet?"

"What's the point of dredging it up?" He stops pacing and levels his gaze on me. "The media would have a heyday. You met Francis. You saw how he moved in the world, how he treated people. Write about the Francis you knew."

"That's all I *can* do, rabbi."

"Come. Your room's just down this hall."

◆

I lie awake with nothing but the dim glow of a streetlamp by which to orient my turnings. From the next room comes a high broken sob, muffled, then Reyn's voice asking, "What did she want to know?'

Mark's response is barely audible. "Everything. Go back to sleep."

"She's upset you, hasn't she?"

"I'm all right, it's just... the finality of it. I wasn't the brother I wish I'd been, and now it's too late."

An unsparing stripe of light falls between my eyes and I rouse, checkered sheets in disarray, my chilled limbs trapped within them. A chink in the blinds reveals white sky, sooty brick. The room is not immediately familiar, but the bookshelves, sagging beneath the weight of Calvary and revelation, confirm my whereabouts, as does the oversized T-shirt I wear, silk-screened with the words *AIDS Network of Greater Boston.*

I dress hurriedly, smooth back my hair, and open the bedroom door halfway hoping to avoid my hosts until I can examine my face in a mirror and make the necessary amendments. Ten minutes later, having showered and refreshed my lipstick, I descend the staircase and pad in borrowed slippers to the kitchen. There is a bowl of fresh fruit on the table, another of muffins; the *Boston Globe* rests folded beside the single place setting.

"Sleep well?" asks Marc, arriving at the threshold,

pausing there as if he were the guest and I mistress of the house.

"Like a jar of two-penny nails."

Marc, still lingering in the doorway, glances at his wristwatch. "I'm late for an appointment across town—but then, so is everyone else."

"And Reyn?"

"Left for work at the crack of dawn. On foot." Marc motions toward the refrigerator. "Please, help yourself. I'm useless in the kitchen; can't identify, let alone prepare, half of what Reyn brings home."

"Join me in a cup of something?"

"There's tea," he suggests, stepping reluctantly into the room. The scent of his aftershave wafts toward me, subtle with a hint of clove. He has nicked his upper lip shaving and a fleck of blood remains visible. Were it not for his winter pallor and the austerity of his attire, he might be Francis— but I'm staring. Marc turns away, begins fumbling with boxes. "Emperor's Choice, Tummy Tamer, Earl Grey— organic, of course—Triple Ginseng…"

"Whatever you're having."

He sets about the task in silence.

"If you don't mind, I'd like to have a look at Francis' townhouse before I go."

"Bill will let you in. I've left what I could find of my brother's notes in a folder atop the desk; you're welcome to make copies."

"Any correspondence?"

"Francis wasn't much for writing letters."

"How did the two of you keep in touch?"

"He'd stop by—summers, that is. Winters, I'd get a postcard."

"And he lived alone?"

"Yes. Well, mostly."

"The redhead?"

Marc turns to me, his hands overfull. "You don't back off, do you?"

"Your brother was charming, attractive. Some woman was bound to snare him sooner or later. Who was she?"

He frowns, pours, and walks two brimming cups to the table. "Look, I have only a few minutes and this is no trifling topic." We seat ourselves at right angles. He touches a finger to the cut lip. "My brother was no playboy; he had the utmost respect for women. In many ways he was an iconoclast, but where romance was concerned, love, he could be terribly old-fashioned. He courted Sophie, met her parents, asked for her hand. It was all very Fifties. When Sophie died, he didn't just mourn her but set about building a monument to her. He neglected his own work to elevate hers. Then, one night, I invited him to a concert; I thought it would do him good to get out. A chamber group—local, but already of some renown—was playing at the Tsai. *She* was their pianist." He pushes a sugar bowl toward me. "The woman was talented, beautiful, as graceful as her playing; everything a man looks for, I suppose. Francis was 'snared.' He wasn't the only one, apparently." He glances again at his wristwatch then toward the window. "Streets must be cleared by now."

"What happened between them?"

"Francis won her over, or so he thought. They seemed to get on well enough. And then she had to leave on tour. She expected Francis to accompany her, but he had been working on Sophie's retrospective—perhaps retrospective isn't the word. Sophie died so young, after all. Francis had been pulling strings to get her work into the Brooklyn Museum. Timing was critical. He flew to New York to finalize details. End of the affair."

"They had words?"

"No, that's just it. She stopped speaking to him, didn't reply to his letters, vanished. Two months later, Francis heard through friends that she had married." He stands to go.

Abandoning any pretense of etiquette, I lurch into his path. "How did Francis take the news?"

"No one saw much of him for a while, a long while." He tugs at the neck of his bulky sweater. "Well, have a safe trip home. I guess I'll be hearing from you." He tries politely to sidestep me.

"Her name, Marc. I need to know her name."

"The woman's entitled to privacy."

"For research only. I won't reveal it. Promise."

He mulls this over for a moment. "Put yourself in her place, an accomplished musician with a following. The past could only embarrass her. No one should be forced to relive the past." The rabbi, winding a loose thread at his cuff, wavers. "I hold you to your word, Bat. Her name is Helene, Helene Storm. She lives in Back Bay, or did. Now, if you don't mind..."

I step aside. "You've been very helpful, Rabbi Stein"

His voice drifts back, "The innocent have everything to fear."

◆

"Mrs. Storm?" Surely the good rabbi didn't expect me to leave Boston without looking the pianist up. Her number is listed; fame has yet to drive her into seclusion.

"This is she." A cultured voice perfectly tuned.

"I'm a friend of Francis Stein."

A silence as of held breath.

"I'm here in Boston, Mrs. Storm. Near your home, in

fact. Could I possibly stop by for a few minutes?"

"What business could you possibly have with me?" All civility shed, the trained diction acid.

"I thought we might be a comfort to each other. I know you cared for Francis."

"Who are you anyway?" Her panic is audible. "No, don't bother to tell me. Comfort? Francis Stein was nothing to me."

"Are you speaking this way because your husband is at home?"

"Yes—no. How dare you." She hangs up.

◆

William O'Bride, discreetly sucking a breath mint, escorts me to the door of Francis' townhouse. "I'll leave you here," he says, handing me a key. "Rips me up to go inside."

"I'll slide the key under your door when I'm finished, all right?"

"I guess I made an ass of myself the other day, huh?" He sounds not so much repentant as impish. Stalling for time, he leans against the doorframe. "No second chances?"

"Too much on my mind, thanks."

Still he lingers. "If you should have a sudden itch…"

I fit the key in the lock and hurriedly enter, closing the door behind me. My first impression is of space, expanses of empty wall, bare carpet. A leather-topped Deco desk occupies the room's center where the light shines brightest. It's not easy to picture Francis at this desk, in this flat, so far from the Noir's ivory beaches and airy verandahs. On what would he have rested his gaze? There's little to see out the window but frost, bare branches, the red and green flickers of a traffic light.

I step into the alcove that served as Francis' bedroom, feel the sheets—heavy-gauge cotton—comb the closet with its pressed shirts and single row of shined shoes, open and close each bureau drawer. Atop the bureau sits a small, carved box holding a pair of gold cufflinks, a Kennedy half-dollar and a woman's engagement ring, and beside the box a framed portrait of Sophie as she might have looked when Francis courted her.

Finding little of interest, I turn again toward the front room and watch, stunned, as a young woman bundled in knits—knitted cloche, scarf, mittens, leg-warmers—steps through the door and gazes about with obvious curiosity. I make no sound. The intruder walks haltingly to the desk, retraces her steps, and quietly calls, "Is anyone here?"

At last she spots me. "I knocked," she says as if to defend herself.

"Sorry, I didn't hear you. My name's Bat—and *you* are?"

"No one. I mean, we don't know each other." She is even younger than she first appeared, her flushed cheeks poreless, eyes brown and clear.

"If you're looking for Francis…"

"He's not here, right? Not a prob, I'll stop back another time." She glances around the room and quickly reaches for the doorknob.

"So, you haven't heard?"

I point her toward a chair, but she holds fast to the door.

"Are you a friend of Francis? A relative? Do you work for him?"

The young visitor lowers her scarf just far enough to reveal a star of David at her throat. "Are you his wife?"

"No," I say too sharply. "But what brings you here? Was Francis expecting you?"

"Unlikely," she admits. "I've come to solve a mystery."

"Look, I'm sorry to be the one to tell you this, but Francis Stein is dead."

"Dead? But how can that be? I mean, he wasn't all that old."

"How did you know Francis? Have you visited here before?"

"Dead?" she repeats as if she hasn't heard me. "Francis Stein dead. Just like that." Tears stream down her cheeks. Without another word she turns and steps into the corridor.

"Wait!" I call after her. "What did you mean, a mystery?"

Weeping audibly, she half turns. "What does it matter now? He's dead. Francis Stein *dead*."

"Hold on, we need to talk." I grab my coat and follow her out. She begins to run. "Who are you? What did you want with Francis?"

I catch sight of her as she races down the stairwell, the tears still streaming, her chin buried in scarves. She charges through the lobby and out onto the street, not pausing to check the traffic light, car horns honking at her back, her wooly stockings streaked with slush.

"Wait!" I call again.

Helpless, I watch the stranger weave through traffic to the opposite curb, hail a taxi, and ride off, taking her secrets with her.

◆

Logan Airport swarms with people escaping, people returning home. I place myself loosely in the latter category, though home in recent years has become more of a yearning than an address, a place I've yet to find.

Gravitating to a far corner, I take a Walkman from my hand luggage, adjust the headset, turn up the volume: *Money in my pocket but I just can't get no love! Money in my pocket but*

I just can't get no—what was it Francis Stein came looking for on St. Germaine? What was it he found? *Money in my pocket*—how does a man of modest means go through twenty-five thousand dollars in a single month? Wine? Women? Stein was too good-looking, too respectable to pay for sex, but surely his passion fixed on an object (in something other than his fevered dreams).

You, with the smirk on your face—that's right, *you*—bring your hot little ear to my lips and I'll tell you a secret: I knew I had no chance with Stein. I knew it each time I'd approach him at a party and feel him draw into himself. Politely, of course. I've never known a man so scrupulously polite. Late nights alone I loathed him for it.

And then once, recently divorced, a little drunk, I called him at the Noir, called after midnight. He answered, uneasy even before I identified myself.

"Bat Manley? Well, hello."

I had no prepared lines, no excuse for intruding on his solitude. "Haven't seen you for awhile—months, in fact—not that you've missed anything. Bunch of deadbeats this season." I clutched my gin tonic and prayed he'd say something. *Anything.*

"I've never been much of a social animal, but if I've missed your fundraiser I'd be happy to make a donation—you collect for a charity of some sort, don't you? Where shall I send the check?"

He was thinking of the annual raffle for the children's hospital. "That's not what I'm calling about." I set down the glass (my hands had begun to tremble). "I'm calling because... do I need a reason?"

"No, I don't suppose so. It's kind of you."

"I'm not being kind. You've read my columns. I'm anything but kind—do you know what people call me? Bat, the Basher." To my shame, I began to titter. "The *Basher*."

"Are you all right?" he asked.

I pictured him in his hotel room perched on the bed, still in his evening clothes. We would make a handsome couple, Clia insisted. Stein was tall, toned. For a white guy he even moved well. It seemed ridiculous suddenly, unnatural, he alone in that roomy bed, I alone in my narrow one. "You never talk to me. Why is that?"

Another pause. "If I've been rude, rude in any way," he stammered, "I apologize."

"Damn you."

He said nothing, only held the line.

"Why must you make this so hard? You know why I'm calling. You know why…"

"I wouldn't want to presume, but I appreciate your call, truly. It *is* kind of you." He replaced the receiver so softly I did not, at first, realize the connection had been cut.

"Damn you," I said again.

◆

Scrap that last confession. I'm not a character in this story, just a roving set of eyes and ears, witness to others' catapults of faith and self-delusion, to the frayed thread of events tightening about my throat.

"*After refusing to open fire on the protesters, the army allied itself with the opposition in calling for Dunfey's resignation. The ex-Prime Minister is believed to have fled the island in his private Lear jet, taking his wife and hunting dogs with him…*"

"Turn off that radio—what time is it?"

Aunt Marva hovers like a storm cloud. "Over and done. Yah slept tru' it."

My temples throb, assailed by static and the fumes from her Tropical Splendor eau de toilette. I can barely raise my head from the pillow.

"Issa new day!" My aunt's worn hands launch upright from her hips and flurry in the air like a cheerleader's pom-poms. "De kingdom of God settin' down in Calabash."

"Seven in the morning? Mercy."

"Only one casualty has been confirmed…"

"Dat white missionary, the one be makin' so much trouble. Got himself shot, wouldn't yah know. De people rankled so bad even guns couldn't keep dem from outragin'."

"What does a missionary have to do with the Prime Minister?"

"Truelove say Germaine behind dem two. Truelove always been a lickle mutant in de head."

"Don't tell that madman's mixed up in this?"

"Dey makin' ignorant on de question."

"The crowds gathered outside the ministerial palace are calling for Hugo Fey, as they did five years ago when Fey challenged Dunfey on the ballot…"

Marva wags an index finger at the speaker. "De election rigged and everybody know it."

Yes, we knew it, but no one dared to cross Dunfey and his thugs. We weren't starving, after all, weren't in chains. So much easier to content ourselves with handshakes and half-truths. Now, Fey waits in the wings, his scars a reminder of the few stale ideals that once mattered, that might matter again.

By degrees I ease onto my side. Marva, her matronly bulk maneuvering around me like a tugboat, sets about plumping pillows. The floorboards softly creak beneath her weight. I reach for the telephone and watch Marva's thick brows arch to meet her hairline.

"Clia," I respond to the unspoken question. "She would want me to call."

There is no dial tone. The handset lies silent in my palm, an electronic corpse. I shake it, jab at the offending buttons, curse into the receiver.

"Calm yahself, Batty."

A moment later I am on my feet, pulling unmatched items of clothing from hangers, rifling through my hand luggage. Outside, history unfolds like an accordion file crammed with unpaid bills—who will pay? Finding no shoes I dash across the room barefoot and snap-up my car keys. Marva switches off the radio.

"Where yah goin'?" she asks, navigating toward me through a sea of pant legs and handkerchiefs. "Issa holy war out there. Yah clothes all tutti-frutti."

My hand bolts upward to center the collar of my blouse, to smooth the bodice. I catch sight of myself in the bureau mirror: a patchwork of a woman, fevered with intention.

Marva touches her fingertips to my forehead. "Yah catch something up north?"

Staring into the weave of her hand, each tiny crease the size of reckoning, I allow myself to be led back to bed.

◆

A pear, a paperback, an etude played on low… How long have I lain here? I count the days by the aspirin tablets Marva leaves beside my pillow. I am not ill, not in any conventional sense, unless one's thoughts can be considered a virus.

It is Clia I think about as the rhythm of life slows and my eyes scan the ceiling, loping from paint chip to grease stain to shadow and back again. Clia: friend, rival, golden girl, all but deified now. Her face on the local cable channel—its unshakable composure, the studied fraction of a smile—has in a matter of days come to symbolize the new era ushered in by her husband's "Politics of Renewal." If one believes the rhetoric, St. Germaine has shaken off the feather boa of vice and begun her ascent to heaven. Blessed be her cane fields and duty-free shops forever and ever! Blessed be our First Lady, whose honeyed complexion and Irish linen sophistication make us feel almost worthy, almost saved, almost—*Mirror, mirror on the wall, can such a vision of exquisiteness pall?*

◆

My informant calls and without preamble tells me to meet him at the usual place. His impatience tells me he's onto something.

"What have you got for me?"

"Just be there," he replies and hangs up.

In moments I am out the door, careening along the slick, tapering road to the rainforest. The day is overcast. The sea sprawls colorless to all sides. I drive along the coast with the radio on, spurred by the slap of waves, by a reggae beat. When at last I arrive, he is already propped against a palm lighting up a filterless. Two rings of sweat deface his uniform.

"I said 12:15."

I glance at my watch: 12:19. "Cut me some slack, all right. What have you got?"

He drags tight-lipped on his cigarette. "I said 12:15."

"So, flog me."

Staring me down he drags on his cigarette without the least haste and exhales in short, sharp gusts, his spite masked only partially by his martial demeanor. He tosses the smoked-down butt at my feet then reaches slowly into a back pocket. "Your friend Fey has us all punching the time-clock. Thinks he can run the country like a goddam Boy Scout troop." His gun barrel fingers unfold a worn sheet of computer paper. "Have a look."

"What is it?"

"Log of the Yank's last phone calls."

I take the printout from him and immediately recognize Marc Stein's phone number. There are two local calls, brief, to an airline. "What's this one?" I ask, pointing to a Brookline exchange.

"You *do* got a nose for this sort of thing. That is Stein's sorry little secret, a treatment center."

"What sort of treatment center?"

"Rehab. Stein was about to admit himself."

The dreaded relapse?

"Seems the man had a habit to the tune of twenty-five hundred dollars a week; we're talking U.S. dollars."

"Come off it. Stein was no addict."

"Tell that to his dealer. We got him in custody. Poor boy scared to death we going to charge him with murder."

"Did he have a motive?"

"There you go again, Bat, playing detective. Leave the policing to us, all right? The evidence clear as soda water: Stein was heavy into smack." He pauses for effect, his chest thrust out and the sweat stains migrating down his flanks. "What does it matter who stuck the knife in his gut? The police can't be expected to clean up after every druggie come through town. Case closed." He turns to leave.

"Hey, you've been holding out on me. You've had this info—how long? I don't pay for old news."

He winks at me over his cement-slab shoulder. "Dis de cherry on top."

"I'm not impressed."

Trampling gulls' eggs with his black steel-toed boots, he heads toward an unmarked car.

I trail after him. "Hold it! You can't just wash your hands of this. Even if it were true…"

"We got no time fah dopeheads," his voice drifts back. "Call de numbah."

◆

I am still sour-mouthed when a day later the news of Stein's "fatal struggle with hard drugs" hits the *Tattler*, compliments of my successor. There is no time to validate sources before the inevitable call from Kromsky.

"You call yourself a biographer?" the editor goads me. "I've got today's New York Times in front of me."

"So have I."

"So do our shareholders." I can hear him snap something—a pencil? His secretary's neck? "When were you planning to tell me? I mean, do I have a stake here?"

"Until I can verify the facts, it's nothing more than a 10-pt. rumor."

"If you ask me, he was framed. Cops do that sort of thing all the time. Have you spoken to the chief of police?"

The chief of police was last seen huddled between his flat screen TV and Harley Davidson in a hired launch puttering north on a high sea—followed in tight formation by identical launches carrying the mayor of Calabash, Secretary General and Minister of Finance. "Give me a few days. It's hard to get hold of people right now."

"Yeah, I heard you had a coup or something." In the background a nasal voice interjects, *"Revolution every other week down there,"* to which Kromsky retorts, *"I've got my own problems."*

As it happens, St. Germaine's one prior coup occurred in 1947.

"You with me, Bat? Look, the news has created a certain amount of buzz, which can't hurt. I'm just afraid one of the schlock houses will send in a hack and scoop us. We need to outrun them."

"But there hasn't been a proper investigation. What little evidence the police have uncovered looks bad for Stein."

"The addiction stuff? A little human frailty never hurts. Not to worry, half the people who pick up the book will be in recovery from something."

"I'm trying to do a competent job."

"What's the matter, can't take the pressure?"

I would like to ram the receiver through a wall with Kromsky still holding the line. The nerve of the man, presuming to hold a monopoly on mettle. "If quick-and-dirty's what you want…"

"You're a sport, Bat."

He hangs up. The dial tone bleats like a kicked dog.

◆

The bath is scalding hot, my slim volume of Hegel as limp as plankton. How, in fact, does the spirit work, or fail? Something about self-creation—volition, tension, climax… Who was I kidding when I enrolled in grad school? Philosophy is for people who can afford to let chances go by, people like Francis Stein. I submerge myself to the shoulders, then to the chin, holding aloft the words that were Stein's front, the smoke screen wreathing his betrayal. My hands let go. The pages bloat and sink.

◆

"My respects, Mr. Prime Minister. This island has waited a long time for a statesman." Admittedly, my tone falls short. I have left no fewer than a dozen messages for the privilege of sucking up to St. Germaine's latest redeemer.

"Sorry to be so long in getting back to you." Hugo could not sound more distracted.

"And Clia?"

"Fine, thanks."

"Change of digs suit her?"

I hear him shuffle papers. A secretary whispers, *"Ambassador Clench on line two."*

"Just tell me this: your friend Francis, you had to have known about his drug habit. Did you think you could protect him?"

"You're off beam with this, Bat."

"Am I? How do you explain the eyewitnesses who saw Stein buying dope on the street? How do you explain his calls to the treatment center? And why was he in such a hurry to leave the island?"

Hugo hesitates. "The only person who can give you an explanation is Francis and he's… gone. Appearances lie."

"That may be, but I've nothing else to go on. You want to clear your friend? Play your cards. Give me one piece of evidence that proves Francis Stein a paragon of temperance."

I hear him dismiss his secretary. "What's gotten into you, anyway? Defaming the dead your new line?"

"Not every dead man's a saint."

"Who are you? Who the hell are you to judge him? A man spends his whole life trying to do right and you come along and cut him down with your killer pen."

"What if your Yank friend had us all fooled? Wouldn't be the first closet junkie to charm his way into our good graces." I am thinking of my second husband, of his puckish smile, manicured hands, and clandestine trips to the bank. I know better than most the price of misplaced faith. Still, the words are wrong. In the barbed silence that follows, I can hear the cords tighten in Hugo's neck.

"This conversation is over."

◆

Clia calls. Clia, into whose lap life's bounty flows without end. I pace my bought-on-installment nylon pile carpet and picture her in the First Lady's notorious black marble hot tub or lounging in an oceanic four-poster bed. I imagine the immensity about her, room upon room, a bodyguard posted before each door.

"We need to talk," she says, sounding entirely herself, neither more nor less arrogant.

"I thought you'd dropped me. It's been weeks."

"I belong to the public now."

We arrange to meet not at the ministerial palace but in the back room of Clia's Odds and Ends. She has hired a shop girl to oversee the business and to feed the cat. Otherwise, the place hasn't changed: the beaded curtains still sway, the postcard racks creak, and the shelves buckle under their load of month-old tabloids.

Clia arrives late, though not later than usual. A limousine leaves her at the curb and parks nearby. An armed bodyguard stands muscle-bound in the doorway.

"You're keeping well." The least I can say.

"Why so formal?" She opens her arms for a hug and I step gingerly into them. "You feel like cordwood."

"I'm still frozen through."

"You're sweating," replies Clia, openly appraising in her signature white linen suit and cat-eye sunglasses. "Worried about Hugo?" She kicks off her proper beige pumps and sinks into a patched and sagging armchair.

I hesitate a moment before taking the seat opposite her. "Should I be?"

She laughs, a nervous little snicker that does not become her. "You'll not find a more passionate proponent of free speech than Hugo Fey."

"This isn't about free speech, it's about friendship. Your husband has made himself the keeper of Stein's reputation."

"If you're saying that Hugo believes in Francis, believes

in him despite the vile slander lately unleashed upon his memory, yes, that's true. You did too, remember?"

The cat leaps yowling into my lap. "Holy bejesus, the claws on this animal!"

"I must have Belinda call the groomer."

"Belinda?"

A coy shrug of the shoulders. "My personal assistant."

I shunt the feline peril from my lap and lumber out of the caved-in chair. "Cushy life, Mrs. Prime Minister. I suppose Belinda oversees the rest of the staff—hairdresser, chef, astrologer, eunuchs…"

"Lose it, Bat. I married the man I loved. Public service does nothing for a marriage. Hugo and I have already discussed it; he won't be standing for reelection. Maybe it's selfish."

"Don't expect me to be your conscience and stop trying to be mine. Yes, I believed in Stein, once. But how well did I know him? Even you, even Hugo—how close did Stein allow you? You never knew his family, his roots; you never set foot in his home—not that he had much of one. The man was just passing through. Do you know for a fact that he wasn't a dopehead?"

"Do you know that he *was*?" Clia remains seated, on the surface unruffled, but I understand her too well to be misled by the measured affect and flawless presentation.

"The evidence suggests—"

"I don't give a damn what the evidence suggests!" She folds her warring hands in her lap. "Francis Stein was a good man."

"Just one problem: I'm in the business of ferreting out the truth, not of dispensing accolades."

"That tickles me, girlfriend. All those years at the *Tattler*, I suppose you were serving the cause of justice and veracity?"

"It was a job."

The room's far corner is not far enough. Clia's voice tracks me, "You weren't at the salon the last talk Francis gave. He wasn't the zealous crusader anymore. Time had softened him, taken the cutting edge off his words. He spoke about love—you would have thought everything had already been said about love."

"Stein wasn't the innocent you take him for. He'd had his share of women—and girls. One young enough to be his daughter went looking for him at his apartment." The memory of her rosy cheeks and dewdrop eyes brings my blood to a simmer. "Doesn't it bother you that Stein never courted a woman of color? For all that lovey talk you'd think he'd have hooked up with an islander."

Clia, wafting jasmine, glides up behind me. "Don't tell me you're still feeling slighted after all these years?"

"It's not that. We all inhabit a skin; we all lust selectively. People are racist by degrees."

"Stein, an addict? Stein, a racist? You're cooking a case against this man so you can put your name on the cover of a book and tell yourself you've struck a blow for truth, when really—face it, Bat—all you've done is put more gossip on the street. You want to rise above your circumstances? You want a new start? Forget this search-and-destroy book and come work for us."

I edge past her. In forty-four years no one has ever cornered me. "PR's not my line."

"Then go back to school. I've got some savings I won't miss."

"Is this a bribe, Clia?"

"Don't insult us both. We've been friends all our lives."

"We've been friends when it's suited you. When did

you last think to call me? You *belong to the public*. Save your rhetoric for the six o'clock news."

"That's small."

The air between us has grown too heavy to breathe. My voice cuts through it like a dull blade. "Don't think you've got me in your pocket." I turn away, tearing the skein of our shared history, of our never equal woundings. "Thanks for the audience, Mrs. Fey. I need to call my editor."

◆

Letter, postmark Boston:

Dear Bat,

No doubt you have heard by now of the police findings suggesting that Francis had a drug habit and that his murder was a result of "unlawful dealings with persons of ill repute."

I don't believe it. I don't believe it and am saddened beyond measure that my brother's memory should be thus debased.

Worse, I can't disprove it. A lifetime of right acts, the authorities inform me, does not constitute hard evidence. I can only tell you this: Francis paid a high price to regain his self-esteem. Through the worst of his struggle he comported himself— unfailingly—with kindness, dignity and regard for others.

As his biographer, you, more than anyone, have the power to shape how my brother will be remembered. Don't be misled by false witness or surface appearances. Man's nature is full of paradox: what he admires he is also driven to bring down. But you, Bat, with your pen, can resurrect, mend, preserve... if you dare to reach that high.

Forgive me for resorting to Talmudic allusion, but in my

fresh-stirred grief it's the ancient sources that speak to me: "The validity of the words depends on the heart's intention."

Yours truly,
Marc Stein

◆

"I saw yah light on." Marva invites herself in. A scent of cinnamon and coal tar soap accompanies her.

It is two in the morning. Sleepless, if not beyond vanity, I have night cream smeared across my cheeks. My aunt looks as crumpled as her calico apron.

"I was on my way home from yah cousin Leontine. Poor girl got de sweats again."

Her tired eyes probe the parlor where the pages of my confusion—letters, binders, Post-it notes—lay strewn across every surface, defaced here and there by a jot of red marker or errant coffee spill. "Yah been busy."

I shrug.

"Yah cousins asking boutcha." Finding no empty spot upon which to lower her bulk, she stands facing me with arms akimbo. "Dis place a combat zone." She takes me by the cloth of my robe and tugs toward the bedroom. I attempt to deter her. "More of the same in there," but she pokes her head across the threshold and sighs.

I clear a corner of the bed, and she drops down like a sinker. "I'll come back tomorrow, Batty, help yah pick up."

"Not yet. There are complications… details I need to sort out."

Worry lines crisscross my aunt's broad brow. "That mahn Stein, I wish he nevah came to de island. Oh sure, he have a heart—don' go defending him—but what good did he bring us islanders? One more ugly headline? One more stain we can't nevah wash away."

"But he did come."

"They come, they all come. And go." She waves a hand toward some invisible border. "It's we got to hold de island together." She sounds like one of Hugo's speeches, like a slogan one would like to believe but no longer can.

"I've been thinking I might go north again."

"Yah shouldna gone de first time." She labors to her feet, bunches the calico apron in both fists. "Yah got no place on de mainland, no family."

"But I can't breathe here with everyone pressing up against me. A person's entitled to a little distance—from the past, from her own mistakes. I don't belong anymore."

Marva lays a warm crinkled hand against my cheek, holds it there, tacky with cream, waiting to catch the tears that won't jar loose.

"Do the dead hear us, Auntie? Do they look down and watch us tear pieces from their memories?"

For once she has no answer. "Sleep now."

◆

I have a date with a saint. Germaine, ensconced in the township church that bears her name, does not expect me. I am not of her flock. I have seen the icon only from afar, when as a child I would watch the procession pass at Easter and again at Christmas, row upon row of the island's poorest tramping through heat and rain after a gaudy doll. How much more respectable was our brick church with its wooden Jesus—our Jesus, who spoke in Latin, never in tongues.

Did Stein fasten on the saint as he did his other subjects, because he found her pitiable, outcast, a pawn? In life she was all these things; dead she's a holy terror. Her followers have been known to dance themselves into a foaming frenzy. There have been reports of orgy-like rituals stretching from dusk-to-dusk, under-exposed photographs hinting at the supposed excesses. Only Truelove seems to have taken them seriously.

The small chapel, far from beckoning me inside, repels by its multiple coats of glossy yellow paint and red carpet remnants, and as I draw closer, by its cloying scent of sandalwood and sweat. From the doorway I spot the icon, resting upon a low altar covered in synthetic blue satin. A narrow aisle leads to a tiny staircase, which in turn leads to Germaine's crudely fashioned feet.

I set off down this gangplank, steadying myself against the pews to either side, colliding with gumdrop-colored shadows (the windows have been tinted pink and green to resemble stained glass).

Midway I pause and the icon's eyes bore into me. Her painted lips scoff, *You, here? You, who worship nothing save cold, hard fact?*

A plastic saint selling me faith.

Plastic I may be, but what are you made of—newsprint, ink? Flesh you are not. Flesh cleaves unto flesh.

The stench, the heat… I should never have come.

Conscience would have brought you to me sooner or later.

"Damn, not *you* too?"

Out of the dimness limps a hunchback, who might be one more shadow were it not for the turkey feather in her tired and dented hat. "Watch yah tongue, missy." She brandishes a hymnal. "Dis a holy place."

"I didn't see you."

"Dat no excuse. Yah be offendin' sensitive ears." Her lopsided arms gesture toward the saint. "*She* hears us. Jesus got no time fi we so fah from de promise land and de Pope neither. Germaine de one divine bean who wit' us always. Germaine be wit' us so long her skin be turnin'. "

The icon's plastic facing, tempered by age and the elements, has indeed begun to darken. The humidity has kinked her synthetic yellow tresses.

The caretaker limps forward and caresses the icon's weathered hand. "Germaine love de blind and de cripple, de los' sheep, de ugly duck…"

"Who lights all these candles?"

"Wimmin. If it wasn't fi we, dis island be fretted by all de plagues and den some."

"Is there someone I could speak with? A pastor?"

"Tain no pastor—where yah been anyway? Dere only de white preacher an everyone know he dead."

"Isn't that blood on her skirts?"

"Das right." The hunchback says this with her chin raised at the angle of a spout. Facing me with the same imperious air, she extends an upturned palm. "One candle fifty cent, two fi one dollah."

I fish a bill from my purse and light a single candle. At close range the altar reveals carved initials, desiccated lilies, messages left behind on folded scraps of paper. I pocket one the size and shape of a spitball, and keeping my gaze on the doll's painted and re-painted smile, back down the aisle toward a side door.

"Germaine love de poor an' de sickly. She love de low an' de fallen, de widows and de orphans, de lonesome hearted… "

I step out into the glare of high noon. Somewhere between the altar and the exit I have lost the heel of my shoe. Steadying myself against the doorjamb, I unfold the pilfered missive: *Can a man take fire in his bosom, and his clothes not burn?*

◆

Veronique is the sea's flesh, the sun's anchor, the tides' magnet… The poem echoes in memory, there is no switching it off. *Child. Woman. Lost.* Who was she? Where does one begin to search for the wellspring of desire?

◆

And just when I think I see through Francis Stein, that I have stripped away his façade of unassuming heroism and laid bare his hypocrisy, I turn to an overlooked page in his notebooks, to a passage lightly *x*'d out in red pencil, and at once he is an enigma to me all over again:

The doves return to St. Germaine, they return in droves, soft downy clouds of them. History can only sigh. Gone the angry words sprawled in blood, gone the pyres. Before anyone can analyze the phenomenon, proclaim it a hoax, a miracle, salvation, siege; before anyone can invoke a saint or down a shot of rum, awe descends on the island like warm milk.

A lone voice rises on the breeze:
The gentle dove she come back singing, 'Love, love, love…'
The devil pack a bag and take to swimming,
Across the ocean with his pockets brimming,
And the people cry out like a bell ringing, 'Love, love, love!'
Waves lap smooth the bitten shores. Sun filters gentle through a canopy of wings. The people turn up their heads and know they are seeing the reflection of their own dreams. The people look up!

◆

Clia's limousine, parked like a beached white whale in front of my house, gathers the sunlight to its flanks. A chauffeur opens the door and the First Lady emerges with feline self-containment and glides up the path. Glancing furtively up and down the lane, she rings my bell.

"Slumming?" I step back from the threshold and wave her in. "There's callaloo on the stove."

"I can't stay." She steps inside, barely far enough to

clear the welcome mat. I turn, intending to usher her to the parlor, but planted like a Venus flycatcher she grips me by the sleeve of my polo. "Hugo mustn't know we've spoken, understand?"

I nod.

"There's a woman named Sarah, a blind woman. Ask her about Francis."

"How do I find her?"

"Start at the Noir and then try Yam Flats." She glances toward the street, one expensively shod foot already out the door.

"Yam flats? A blind woman? If I didn't know better, girlfriend, I'd think you were sending me fishing in a desert."

Clia indulges me with a measured smile. I watch her glide across the street and enthrone herself on the limo's leather seat. A crowd has assembled beneath the awning of Yvette's Sweet Temptations to cheer as she passes. She has her driver open the rear windows. As the car pulls away she blows kisses, dispensing them like alms from her petal-light hands.

◆

I walk the rutted mud lanes of Yam Flats, asking for Sarah, fingers pointing me here, there, until at last I stand before the scrap-wood door of an unnumbered tin and clapboard cubicle. I knock. The door, listing on slack hinges, gives way. And then I see her: blade thin yet without angles, seated, wrapped from chin to hips in a tattered shawl, a swath of silk hanging limp about her thighs.

"I've been expecting you," she says in a voice at once deep and strikingly female.

I waver on the threshold.

"The batwoman. Your radar may be *précisément précis*, but even you thrash about in the dark."

"Then you know why I've come."

Her blank eyes rest squarely on my face; I cannot put a color to them. "Of course. Hugo's friend, the *petit blanc.* He felt sorry for me, can you imagine? As if *I* were the blind one."

I can't help but look around, though there is little to see—a hotplate, a broom, a caged canary. Every surface wears a layer of dust, every corner a cobweb.

"Busy eyes. Sit down."

Sarah vacates the room's one chair and lowers herself onto a straw pallet, dragging the fringes of shawl after her. "You're going to ask me, who killed the *petit blanc*? Name the murderer, point me toward him. What for? Every man carries the seeds of his own destruction; the *blanc* was no exception."

"Someone stabbed the knife into his hide."

"An impulse. We all have them, even those who wear the gospel like a *camisole de force.* A man with a notion to live stays out of harm's way."

"But he was an addict."

Sarah waves an index finger in the manner of a metronome. "It was she, not he."

"She?" *Stein's fatal muse.*

"By the time he returned to the island, the addiction had hold of her. He gave her the powder the way he had once given her schoolbooks, vitamin tablets. There was never a time she didn't lack for something. Buttons falling from her blouses, and her aunt such a fox."

"Who was she?"

"No one. A girl." The blind woman lets the shawl slip down her shoulders, revealing curvilinear expanses of ochre-tinged flesh. "A girl with bad relations: first the aunt, then the uncle. They were all the kin she had. Once the aunt left the island, her brother—a small-time pimp out to expand his stable—took over the girl's 'education.' A vulture couldn't have asked for easier prey, so hungry and her head full of froth. The *petit blanc* thought he could save her. There is something of the messiah in every Jew. Get the girl off the island, I told him, but he waited too long."

"Her own uncle? He went after Stein and the girl?"

"Not that simple, life is no whodunit."

"But I need to know. It was the uncle, wasn't it?"

"The question is not who did it, the question is—"

I take her hand with its gold and silver rings and thrust a wad of bills into the unresisting palm. "*I* frame the questions, all right?"

"You think you can buy the truth like a morning paper?" The bills disappear into her flaccid cleavage. "Ask what you like. Sink your little rodent teeth into the scum of a dead man's good intentions. And if you must know, it wasn't Uncle Pimp who found the girl; *she* called him." Sarah pauses as if to gauge my reaction. "She didn't trust strangers. The *petit blanc* had to be making fun of her somehow—how else to explain his generosity? He didn't sleep with her, after all. Such was her reasoning, if the twisted thoughts of a ruined girl can be called reason."

A scorpion scuttles down the broom handle.

"She regretted it, of course, but too late. She hadn't counted on the *blanc's* audacity—what did she know about character? The drug clouded what little judgment she had."

"But she lured Stein, to his death."

"You are too hard on the creature. The girl had no intention of getting the *blanc* killed. One can't blackmail a dead man, after all."

"Blackmail? But Stein gave willingly."

"The more reason to despise him. Do you know

nothing about the *bête humaine?*"

Assailed by the blind woman's fathomless eyes, I can almost feel glad of my ignorance.

"She got the idea from a book, of all things." Sarah appears to laugh, though no sound emits from her wound of a mouth. "The perfidy of the written word! The fool was always taking her books."

"But *who* was she?"

"I told you, she was just a girl."

"Can you take me to her?"

Again the fleshly metronome. "Gone. We'll never find her."

"And Uncle Pimp?"

"Biding his time on the mainland. He'll be back; the bad ones always come back."

I stand, circle the chair, and brace against its wooden frame. "Not a single witness. I can just hear Kromsky now, 'Give me a story, give me something real, give me, give me, give me…'"

Sarah yawns. "*Eh, bien?*"

"Stein's notebooks, he was writing something."

"Island life stood on end the *blanc's* notions of right and wrong. The religiosity of our passions, the violence of our piety! What a quandary we posed, what an irresistible coil of contradictions." Again she yawns, clutches absently at the meager folds of her nightdress.

"You exaggerate."

"Not at all. A congregation locks themselves in a chapel and sets the place ablaze. One might very well blame it on the white preacher, scaring them half out of their wits with apocalyptic claptrap, but it was the people who struck the match. They might have saved themselves—the tin walls were no thicker than a holy wafer—but instead they danced.

They danced…"

"What does that have to do with Stein?"

"We forced open his eyes, tore away his illusions. Why else did he ask whose arm shall thrust us under in the end, God or man's?"

She turns her back, leaving the riddle unanswered. I would like to shake her.

"So, which is it?"

She laughs open-mouthed. "A trick question. One is as tossed-about as the other. The ultimate danger is, has always been, the widening chasm between heart and hand. The *petit blanc* had already figured that much out."

The day's last light recedes like a yellow tide. Twilight streams in.

"You are not satisfied."

Forgetting she can't see me, I nod.

"You doubt."

"Yes."

"Then close your eyes. Close your eyes and listen."

I take a step forward in protest. The soothsayer waves me away and stretches out on the pallet, her sightless eyes fixed on a chink in the metal roof and the first drops of rain sleeting through it. "You wanted a story. *Listen…*"

FRANCIS

Eleven-fifty and the clock of impossible hopes keeps on ticking. I step to its beat, kick away the shattered glass, the streamers, steer toward the rainbow houses aglow like paper lanterns above a slapping sea giddy with stars. A pandemic of mirth sweeps through Calabash. The women laugh from too much rum, they reel, their faces flushed, their men off wandering.

Jubilation, good people! The moment of moments is upon us and everywhere the music blaring, *God bless the children, God bless the children because they can't stop what men do...*

So little time left.

I insert my key in the door of the leaning house and find it unlocked. Cooking smells drift out to greet me. A dim glow emits from underneath the bedroom door—could she be reading at this hour? Or is she waiting for midnight, for the familiar tumult of church bells, car horns, firecrackers...

the anticlimax and gradual return to sameness.

I expect her to call my name, as she always does, but there is only the muffled din of someone else's celebration. Not wanting to startle her, I call softly, "Are you awake?"

A rustling of bedclothes. "Veronique?" My hand presses against the bedroom door and it opens without resistance.

"Yah come to de wrong place, mistuh Stern," says a very naked man, lounging in bed beside her with a hand clamped to her waist. He feigns a yawn, flaunts his filed white teeth. "De Yank pahty down de street where all de lights shinin'."

"Veronique?"

She lowers her eyes, draws the bed sheet up over her breasts, but not high enough to cover the blue glitter of necklace at her throat. Her bedmate intercepts my gaze. "Yah been hanging 'round my wumman, but she not be needin' yah no way. I be takin' she back now." He hooks one enormous thumb under the gold chain and snaps it in two. Veronique shrinks into the pillows, her chin twitching and a forefinger lamely palpating the spot where the gemstone had once cooled her skin.

I step into the room, aware suddenly of the plates on the bedstand; she has fed the man the remains of our Christmas dinner. She has folded his Sergio Valente bluejeans over the footrest. Her red shoes lie beside the bed, the left one housing a used syringe.

The stranger sits up. "Dat far enough, Stern."

I can't resist the urge to take another step, if only to rankle him. "This isn't your home. She isn't chattel. Who the hell are you, anyway?"

He folds his arms, drawing my eye to the double viper tattooed on the biceps.

"I see."

He almost smiles. "Yah don' see nuthin."

I take another step and watch with morbid fascination as the naked man, who I shall henceforth call the Viper, swivels his muscular torso toward me and drops his long hard legs over the side of the bed.

"Veronique, don't lose your voice now. Be your own heroine."

Her blue-black eyes sweep toward me, unfocused, round with terror. "Yah get out, *François.*"

"You don't have to do this—"

"Get out!"

The Viper plucks a morsel of black cake from one of the plates and stuffs it into his mouth. "Yah heard de lady," he says, licking crumbs from his fingers with a greedy tongue. Then I notice his penis, dangling with insouciance between his woolly thighs. A final provocation.

"You sonuvabitch! Look what you've done to her." I lunge forward and kick the whore-red shoes across the floor. "Look at her. She can't get through a day without stabbing dope into her veins. By the time you're through with her, she'll have no more choices. No future. Nothing."

"Bettah she be a black mahn's livelihood than a white mahn's slut."

It is hard to say what happens next, if lightning flashes in the sky or the barrel of a '45 glints above my head, if the woman-child screams or the tower clock chimes midnight… and perhaps all these things happen at once, too quickly to register. She is screaming freely now, but no one hears her. The New Year comes in with a great noise, smothering her cries. I would like to press my lips to her lips, to breathe her breath; there is no air in the little room and the Viper, more imposing for his nakedness, is wrestling me out into the street—"Time yah get on."

Behind him I can see her clutch at her ribs, which bare of flesh obtrude like the tines of a pitchfork. A parting glance and the door slams closed.

I stand in the street watching revelers dance past the windows, raise their glasses, toast, slip onto porches to piss in the shrubbery… another year gone by. Time to get on. *God bless the children, God bless the children…* A few tentative steps and I feel an arm steady me, a woman's arm, soft-skinned, the wrist wafting patchouli.

"All alone?" Clia's friend from the Tattler, whose name I cannot put my tongue around just now.

"Happy New Year," I say, all the encouragement she needs to lean over and kiss me wetly on the lips.

"These silly parties." She tugs me gently to another of the leaning houses, hers, which is pink and has a pair of bougainvillea in the front yard. She does not let go my arm. "I can use a nightcap—how about you?"

"If you'd like the company."

She opens the pink door and nudges me ahead of her toward a tidy kitchen with mermaids on the wallpaper. "You're being polite," she scolds me. "Make yourself comfy. Rum okay?"

It is all she has. She leads me to a sofa and sits down beside me, close, an invitation.

"You have a lovely place," I compliment her. It reminds me of a sweet shop—candy pink walls, chocolate upholstery.

"Don't feel that you need to make small talk. I'm just glad you're here."

"It's kind of you to invite me."

Her nose crinkles. "There you go again. Relax. I'm off-duty." She clinks her glass against mine, hard, and the pale gold rum spatters onto her bodice. "I don't expect to be courted. This isn't prom night."

"You're a beautiful woman." Of the Amazon type, handsome rather than pretty.

"Am I? It's taken you a while to notice—ten years? Twenty?"

"Have we known each other that long?"

"I suppose I owe you an apology, that awkwardness some time back… I'm not always—subtle."

"Forgotten."

"Fresh start then?" She turns strangely coy, casting down her eyes and arranging the folds of her skirt. "Truth be told, I had given up on you. But here we are. How did you know where I live?"

"I didn't. I was in the neighborhood."

Her black whip of a brow arches only to fall. "Then the rumors are true? You've got a mistress hidden away."

"No, no…"

"So, what's stopping you?" She sidles closer, tongue extended like a poisoned dart.

"You may as well know," I feel obliged to tell her, "I'm leaving St. Germaine. For good this time."

She sips audibly at her drink. "A last night. I'm the queen of last nights." In one feline pounce she snatches the glass from my hand and swings her not-insubstantial legs across my lap. Her voice goes breathy. "Nothing to stop us then, is there? I'll even drive you to the airport."

"You deserve better than that."

Her eyes fix on mine. "What are you made of, Francis Stein?"

"Please, I'm just a man."

"Are you?"

She undoes the pearl buttons of her blouse, not all of them, a tease, and I list onto her bosom, bury myself in the perfumed flesh to suckle and maul—what other men do. She moans and her hand springs on reflex to knead my groin.

"Not like this. If you ever find yourself in Boston... we'll see each other again."

To my relief she doesn't cling, only murmurs, "Right."

"Don't trouble yourself to see me out."

She waves a hand toward the door: I am free to go.

Outside the women wear high-heels on their hands and walk barefoot, their buttocks marking time to the music. Paper streamers snake along the gutters. A bull-chested man in uniform steps out from the police station and empties his revolver in the air. I head for the cane fields, for the cliffs, where I might escape the pandemonium and let the salt breeze lick my face. I move to the beat of a hundred calypsos, each one blasting from a different doorway. Tonight all the doors of the world are open! Nothing can keep out the music.

No less a melody is the voice at my back, so soft I might be imagining it: "White devil!"

I glance over a shoulder expecting to see a child, a pack of children, waiting to hear their laughter, but music is what I hear, shadows what I see, dusky purple, mottled blue. A cat dives from a stump and rakes its claws across the sand.

"White devil!" Closer now, accompanied by a low wheeze.

I keep walking.

"White devil! Tain yah place."

"Edwin Truelove?" I say, turning. "Truelove, I've been wanting to talk to you."

Without his sandwich sign the mestizo looks diminished, unnaturally narrow, a dark beanstalk of a man with oiled tufts of hair that gleam in the dark. "I not be talkin' ta yah kind."

"You must be confusing me with someone else—a

missionary? I'm not a missionary."

"Yah kind all be sellin' de same bale of straw." He staggers sideways, drunk probably, one hand palpating the air for a grip, the other cached behind his back "White devils, all of yah…"

I lunge torward him hoping to break his fall, but I misjudge the distance, overrate my own agility, and we glance off each other like dinghies in a gale.

"Yah took me wife," he mutters.

"Brother, I'm sorry for your loss."

"Don' be callin' me bruddah! De devil have a thousand faces."

From behind his back the shy arm jolts into view then seems to vacillate, searching for a target. I watch, mesmerized, as it swoops down toward my stomach (not without grace) and stabs something silvery into me. Moonbeams gather there. Truelove wheezes, whimpers and slowly, slowly backs away. "Find yahself a doctuh."

I look down and see the knife's hilt protrude above my belt like an added appendage.

"Hospital up de road." He gestures north, south, all the while putting distance between us—or perhaps the distance was always there, waiting to be made flesh.

I feel no pain. To the contrary, a slow-acting euphoria is working its way up my solar plexis.

"Don' be lookin' at me," Truelove pleads, "I can't save yah." He gestures south, north. He anchors the errant hand to his side, veers, and staggers off, his luminous hair ebbing like the tail of a comet.

Not a soul in sight. No reason to linger. Slack in the joints I unbutton my suit jacket (the wind makes it billow) and tug loose my tie. As my feet drag through the scrub, crickets shelter in the ferns.

The wind gusts and I blow to that stretch of fallow land dotted with squatters' huts, where an orphaned girl once lived with a wicked aunt. Where she read her first books and ingested whole an era, a language, a hereditary nobility not her own, and dared to dream. The hut is still there. An old man in pajama bottoms sits on the porch eating from a can.

Up ahead, rising out of the sand like a mythic citadel, stands the Noir wearing all the adornments of the season— wreathes, tinsel, colored lights. Her radiance draws me irresistibly. I am ready now for that second glass of champagne.

I approach bleeding though no one seems to notice; as the blood trickles down, my dark pants absorb it. My jacket occults the knife hilt. The doormen, dozing on their feet, part to let me through. The lobby lies empty. The ballroom doors have been propped open with planters, and inside, the lights dimmed to resemble twilight. People have merged into one perfumed, sweat-drenched body swaying to a rhythm of congas and ceiling fans. A singer in leather hip-huggers belts out, *Money in my pocket but I just can't get no love, money in my pocket but I just can't get no*—love?

With bubbles tickling my throat I resolve, starting tomorrow, to write the definitive work on the subject, the tablet that will point the way once all the false idols have toppled. But that is tomorrow, a long time off. Tonight I dance! I shall be one with this grinding mass of flesh and rum and despair... perchance to forget, but that is not likely.

And now a face hovers over me, familiar and yet not. *C'est vous, Monsieur Blanc?* All these years I thought you a figment, an absence. Yet here you are, unabashedly human and so near I can see a razor burn on your cheek.

"Does it hurt?" The pain you suppose is already etched on your brow. Your commanding hands hang as limp as cutlets at your sides.

Aren't you going to clap? You are so still, so drained of volition. I can smell your mortality.

"An ambulance will be here any moment, Mr. Stein. Just hang on, hang on…"

I would like to say, don't trouble yourself. I would like to say—*how bright it is suddenly! What a perfect beginning.*

BAT

Crowds rim the Hotel Noir, those same onlookers who only days ago were shooed from her beach, too threadbare or drunk to mingle with the tourists, their music an affront, their sweat unclean. Today all is celebration. Boom boxes blare. The wrecking ball maneuvers into place at the hotel's sun-blasted flank, and for a moment the stateliness of her columns, of her stacked balconies, stills the commotion. A baby cries.

I take my place, suitcase in hand. I take my place, one more pair of eyes rabid to see the past topple.

A voice cries out, "Let she have it!" and the ball rears back.

The first strike cracks open the western wall, laying bare the ballroom stripped of its crystal chandeliers, the galley below gutted, a palm sacrificed, and the crowd swelling with applause.

"Why do they cheer?" asks the young woman beside me.

I glance at her. Red-haired, fair-skinned, she too holds a suitcase.

"People like to see things fall down," I tell her. "Spirit of the times."

The ball strikes again, making pieces of the verandah, the marquee, bringing down the flagpole.

The girl's chin quivers. "I came too late."

Something about her sorrow makes me take a closer look. "Haven't we met?"

"You? Here? Long haul from Boston."

The clue that got away. "I never did catch your name. But tell me, did you solve your mystery?"

She laughs so softly it might be the sound of a tide ebbing. "What else would have brought me to this island? My father used to stay here... before."

And then her puppy-brown eyes brim over, oddly familiar eyes.

"Francis Stein?"

"I found letters, letters he'd sent to my mother Helene Storm—the pianist? Not long before I was born."

"Then your mother never told you?"

"Never told, and never forgave." Her soft white hand reaches out to me, timidly brushes the sleeve of my traveling dress. "You're the woman who wrote that book, aren't you? Did you know Francis well?"

She is an arresting synthesis of her mother's fiery mane, her father's stature, and a sadness so affecting I feel my own composure slip. The ball rises for another swipe.

"No, not well."

I cannot hear her reply above the hurrahs and music, above the babies' frightened sobs. She turns her gaze from the wrecking ball, sets down her suitcase, and cups hands to her ears. The tremor passes.

"I wrote the book to try and puzzle him out." She looks so crestfallen that I hasten to add, "To us islanders Francis Stein was a sort of prophet. He knew us better than we know ourselves. He'll never leave us. The beat agrees with him—he said that once."

"Anyway, I liked the book."

"Then it was all worth it." The self-doubt, the secret keeping, Kromsky's wrath… what would I not have endured to keep faith with Francis Stein? "Winters won't be the same without your father. What I would have liked more than anything was to sit with him and have a long talk. Just to talk with him."

"Me, too."

She half smiles and moves off, the suitcase hoisted onto a shoulder and her unbound tresses trailing on the breeze like flame. The water draws her. She steps out of her canvas shoes. I watch her make her way along the beach, a lissome figure, remote and more remote, a sunbeam on the horizon.

The Hotel Noir falls and keeps on falling. What mysteries lie buried beneath her rubble, what warped bones of truth? Stray dogs do their business in her ruin of a lobby. Hornets nest in her listing eaves. When nothing remains but a skeleton of steel girders, the wind changes and the detritus blows out to sea, sinks slowly beneath the waves like flotsam. Finding nothing to loot, the crowd tosses its beer cans and disperses. A moon the color of waking and so big it makes me shudder rises from the spindrift. With salt lashing my lips, I take up my burden and walk back the way I came.

Acknowledgments

How does a pseudonymous author acknowledge friends and supporters without indulging in a literary "dance of the seven veils?" Those of you who know my true identity will, I hope, recognize yourselves in this necessarily cryptic tribute.

To all the people I have thanked in prior books, please know that you remain dear to me, and the reason I persevere as a writer despite all. To old friends I may have overlooked (we both know who you are), forgive me, for I am no less flawed than the characters I create. To new friends, please watch for your name in my next directly authored book.

Without malice or sarcasm I thank the agents and editors who have rejected my work along the way and made me reach higher. I also thank those who, like Pale Fire Press, have had faith and joined me on a leg or two of the circuitous journey toward publication and beyond.

Finally, I thank the characters in this book for being such droll and illuminating company during the writing, and my readers for filling the vacancy left once the players exit the stage. It is your book now. With gratitude and love I place it in your hands.